Also by Francis King

The Sunlight on the Garden

About the Author:

Francis King is a former International President of PEN and drama critic of the *Sunday Telegraph*. His fiction includes *Act of Darkness, Dead Letters* and *The Custom House*. Arcadia published *Prodigies* to great acclaim in 2001, while his 28th novel *The Nick of Time* was longlisted for the Booker Prize 2003, attracting critical praise from Harold Pinter, Antonia Fraser, Beryl Bainbridge, Penelope Lively and Margaret Drabble.

The Sunlight on the Garden

Stories

by

Francis King

A

ARCADIA BOOKS
LONDON

Arcadia Books Ltd
15-16 Nassau Street
London W1W 7AB

www.arcadiabooks.co.uk

First published in the United Kingdom by Arcadia Books, 2005
Copyright © Francis King 2005

A catalogue record for this book is available from the British Library.

ISBN 1-900850-99-0

Typeset in Bembo by Basement Press, London
Printed in the United Kingdom by J. W. Arrowsmith Ltd. Bristol

Arcadia Books distributors are as follows:

in the UK and elsewhere in Europe:
Turnaround Publishers Services
Unit 3, Olympia Trading Estate
Coburg Road
London N22 6TZ

in the US and Canada:
Independent Publishers Group
814 N. Franklin Street
Chicago, IL 60610

in Australia:
Tower Books
PO Box 213
Brookvale, NSW 2100

in New Zealand:
Addenda
Box 78224
Grey Lynn
Auckland

in South Africa:
Quartet Sales and Marketing
PO Box 1218
Northcliffe
Johannesburg 2115

Arcadia Books: *Sunday Times* Small Publisher of the Year 2002/03

For Quentin
for all his encouragement and help

Contents

Mouse

Derek Hammond would always call me Mouse.

From the top of the steps he would shout down into the steamy changing-room, with its smells of sweat, chlorine and carbolic soap, 'Mouse, Mouse, where the hell are you?' Everyone would look up at him and then across at me. The general laughter that followed was as though all of them were flicking at my naked body with their damp towels – a humiliation that they often inflicted on me.

He would hold up a slice of toast: 'Oh, Mouse, Mouse, Mouse! Can't you possibly concentrate long enough not to incinerate every slice of bread you get your grubby paws on?'

He would loom above me: 'I'm afraid I'm going to have to beat you, Mouse. This is the third time you've been the last person to leave the study and have forgotten to turn off the light.' His voice would be jolly, he would be smiling. After the beating he would say: 'Sorry for that, Mouse.' Once he added: 'It's all for the good of your soul, you know.'

When I told my widowed mother how much I hated to be called Mouse, not merely by him but, in derisive imitation, by the other boys in my year, she said: 'Oh, but that's just affectionate.'

'No, no, it isn't.'

'Of course it is. The trouble is that you're always so touchy. Your father often used to call me Little Rat. That was affectionate too, of course it was. And a rat is a far less attractive creature than a mouse. Mice are sweet little things.'

I did not want to be a sweet little thing. In any case, she had not convinced me. The trouble was that I looked like a mouse. I was diminutive for my age. My eyes were tiny and bright, with pink rims, my nose was long and pointed, my ears were far too large, and I had virtually no chin. I hated my appearance, just as, unwillingly, I admired and envied his. If I was like a mouse, he was like a lion, golden, lithe and strong.

I was his fag for only a year. That was the length of any new boy's servitude. In any case, he had then moved on, first to read PEP at Oxford and then, after the outbreak of the War, to join Fighter Command as a pilot. At the end of the last day on which I was at his peremptory beck and call, he inspected the shoes that I had polished for him and declared, in the jocular, vaguely jeering tone now so familiar to me: 'Oh, Mouse, Mouse, I have an awful feeling that you've used black polish, not brown.' He held out one of the shoes. 'Look, Mouse. Bloody *look!*' Suddenly the lion sprang off the chair in which he had been lolling. With the hand that was not holding out the shoe he grabbed me by the scruff of the neck and thrust my head downwards. 'Look, blast you, you little twerp!' The hand released me and ruffled my hair. He laughed. 'What's to become of you, Mouse? You're absolutely hopeless.' I did not answer, biting my lower lip as, red-faced, I stared down at my feet. I felt myself to be, not for the first time in his presence, on the verge of tears.

'Oh, well, never mind. I have something for you. A present. Not that you deserve it, Mouse. No one can ever have had to put up with quite so useless a fag. What do you think about all the time?' He had asked me that question on many other occasions. 'That bally thumping of yours? Do you really think that you're going to become another Rubinstein or Solomon? You're far more likely to end up playing for dancing classes at a girls school. Oh, Mouse, Mouse, Mouse!' He gave a theatrically exaggerated sigh. 'Well, never mind. It takes all sorts.' He drew out his wallet. It was made of crocodile leather, a gift, he had once told me, from an uncle who had made a fortune in the meat trade in Argentina. His dream was to go out there for a while – oh, not to make money, but to play polo, he said.

'Here you are, Mouse! Not that you deserve it.'

To my amazement it was a large, white £5 note. Such a note had never been seen in the impoverished household of my mother and myself. She had once told me that, if one used such a note, one had to endorse it, like a cheque, before it was valid.

I shrank away, as though from something contaminated. I could not believe that he was giving me so large a sum. My uncles never tipped me more than ten shillings; usually I had to be content with a florin or a half-crown from them.

'Come on! What's the matter? Haven't you ever seen a five-pound note?'

Mutely I put out my hand.

'Well, there you are, Mouse. You've been an awful trial to me, but you're not a bad little squirt. Perhaps you'll improve.'

'Thanks. Thanks a lot.' Looking down at it, I began to uncrease the note between the fingers of both hands.

I used the money to buy some second-hand piano scores from a murky, dusty, labyrinthine shop in Charing Cross Road to which I often used to go when I had any cash. During the Blitz, the shop, all its stock, the proprietor and his elderly woman assistant, who hobbled around with an iron brace on her right leg, were all to be annihilated by a bomb.

Five years later I was walking my mother's spaniel, Roy, in Kensington Gardens. This was a task that my mother, mysteriously to me, enjoyed and claimed for her own. But she had had a fall in the black-out, while returning from her work as an auxiliary nurse at St Mary Abbot's Hospital, and was now laid up with a sprained ankle. Roy, who was almost as old as I was, was exasperating me, as always, with his slow, panting progression from one tree to another, first to sniff and then laboriously to cock a rheumatic leg and emit a slow trickle of bronze-coloured urine. I tugged on the lead but, obstinate, he would not budge.

Suddenly, Roy froze and jerked up his head. A moment later, I too heard the churning of a V1. That sunny afternoon the Gardens were full with people in their Sunday best – many of the men in dark suits, most of the women in hats. At the approaching noise, almost all of them flung themselves down either on the pathway or on the grass. I remained standing, tugging at Roy.

Soon I realised that, in charge of a wheelchair, a tall, elegant woman was also standing – not far from me, in the centre of the same path along which I had been dragging the dog. In an instant, as I waited for the V1 to detonate, I took in the beautifully tailored grey suit, the grey gloves, the pale-pink blouse and the pale-pink hat, its brim tilted at a jaunty angle up and away from the face.

I then heard a voice, unmistakable to me. 'Mouse! *Mouse!*' Irrationally, I at once felt the same trepidation that I did when I used to hear it back at school. The voice was coming from the wheelchair. My first emotion was one of astonishment. I had thought the figure slumped in it to be an old man.

As I stared in incredulity, the V1 passed over with a now diminishing splutter. The splutter ended in the muffled thump of its impact on what I later learned was a block of Knightsbridge flats. All the people who had been lying on the lawn or the path, now scrambled to their feet and began nonchalantly to dust themselves down. The women straightened their hats, one even taking a mirror out of her bag and peering into it as she did so. In recollection the scene has now become a comic one for me. At the time, it was merely a humdrum part of wartime life in London.

'Mouse! Come over!' With a mixture of bewilderment and dread, I had been hesitating. Slowly I walked towards the wheelchair. 'Don't you recognise me?'

Of course I could not reply: 'You've changed out of all recognition.' So I did not venture an answer. He had had large, strong hands, the nails of which, unusual for a schoolboy, he had always scrupulously manicured. Now they were like the talons, stiff and striated with purple and black, of some dead bird of prey. I took in the face. One side was crimson and hideously rucked up and there was a pink celluloid eye-patch over the eye. Even on that summer's day there was a tartan rug reaching from his waist to his ankles.

'How strange to meet you here! I've often wondered what happened to you.' His voice had always been forceful. Now it was little more than a hoarse whisper. He turned his head upwards with a brief grimace, as though it hurt him to do so. 'Ma – this is Mouse.' I felt a spasm of fury. Why did he have to use that derisive nickname after so long time? 'You remember my talking of Mouse?'

'Yes, of course, I do. Hello, Mouse.' She raised her hand from the wheelchair and held it out to me. My first impression was of her narrowness. The pale face was narrow, with the grey-green eyes set close together, and the waist, legs, ankles and feet were all narrow. 'Was he a terribly demanding taskmaster? I'm sure he was. He has no patience.' Later, I was to see many examples of this lack of patience in his treatment of a woman who, however urgent the job in hand, never herself hurried.

'Well, what are you up to? You must have left the old place by now.'

'Oh, yes, a year ago.'

'Did you make house prefect?' He laughed. 'I bet you didn't.'

Humiliated, I shook my head. I might have added: 'But I'm the youngest person ever to have played at a National Gallery concert.'

'And now?'

'I'm up at Oxford. Balliol. I got a music scholarship.' I almost added that, but for the scholarship, I could never have gone there.

'No call up? Don't tell me you're a pacifist. That would be entirely in keeping with all I remember of our Mouse.'

'No. Asthma. I have this asthma.'

'Oh, Christ, yes! How you used to gasp and wheeze!' His face cracked into a lop-sided smile, the mouth twisting upwards. 'Well, you can see the sort of state I'm in. No more bloody use. Shot down,' he added bleakly.

'You're going to be back on your feet in no time at all.' His mother spoke with a desperate attempt at conviction that could not fool me and certainly could not have fooled him. 'They're quite confident about that.' She was always to speak of the doctors and nurses as 'they'.

'So it's now the vacation?'

'That's right. But I must get a job.'

'*Must?*'

'My scholarship doesn't stretch all that far.' Though I did not want it to be, my tone was resentful. That tone said: 'You've never had to worry about money for a single moment. My mother and I have to worry about it all the time.'

'What sort of job are you looking for?' Lady Hammond asked.

'Oh, anything. I thought I might get some tutoring. Music would be best. That's the only thing I'm good at.'

'So you still want to be another Rubinstein or Solomon?' Hammond interposed.

I did not answer. It was the same affectionate yet jeering tone that I remembered from those already remote days when I had been his slave.

Lady Hammond tilted her head, the sunlight glinting on the ornamental silver buckle at one side of her pink hat. 'I might think of something,' she said. 'You wouldn't want to do farm-work, I imagine. If you did, I could ask our bailiff.'

'Mouse would be no bloody use at farm-work. He was always hopeless at anything practical.'

'Let me have a think about it.' She opened the bag hitched to one of the handles of the wheelchair and drew out what looked, at first glance, like a small silver cigarette case. Attached to it was a pencil, also silver, almost as slim as a matchstick. She opened the cover of the case and then passed both it and the pencil over to me. 'Give me your address. On that pad inside. Oh, and also add the telephone number. Do you live in London?'

'Yes, not far from here. ... Stop it Roy!' He was tugging impatiently at his lead. It was difficult to write with one hand while the other attempted to restrain him.

'Let me have him while you're writing.'

I disentangled the lead from my wrist and she took it from me.

'Now stop that! Sit! *Sit!*' Amazingly Roy at once obeyed her. He stopped jerking at the lead and moved close against one of her legs, his head raised to look up at her with those eyes that my mother called soulful and I thought merely sloppy. He was never as obedient as that with my mother, much less with me.

'Well, it was good seeing you, Mouse. You haven't changed at all. Except that you're much bigger now. The mouse could now almost pass for a rat.'

'Do you know my son's companion?' That was how Lady Hammond would introduce me to visitors or people encountered when we were out together. But I was far more than merely a companion. Perhaps she thought that, by ignoring that fact, she allowed me to retain my dignity. All too often – since the staff at the Hall had been so much reduced by the war – I was also nurse, messenger, butler and valet. As I practised at the sadly out-of-tune Bechstein piano in the music room, I would hear the thumping of Hammond's stick on the ceiling above me. As I wandered across the overgrown croquet lawn, I would hear, from the open window beneath which his daybed had been placed, his imperious 'Mouse, Mouse, *Mouse!*' Sometimes he wanted me to 'nip down' (as he usually put it) to the village store for the Senior Service cigarettes at which he constantly sucked with desperate greed. Sometimes I had to perform some more intimate duty for him – hauling him on and off the commode, fetching him the urine bottle and then emptying it, or sponging down his once athletic and now emaciated and shattered body. So far from showing any gratitude for these services, they would all too often make him irritable. 'Oh, you're so clumsy!' he would exclaim, writhing under my hesitant touch. 'Oh, do call Nanny!'

Nanny had first been nanny to Lady Hammond. She had then become nanny to Hammond, an only child. Now that Hammond had physically regressed to babyhood, she had once again become nanny to him. By the time that I met her, she must have been in her eighties, a tiny, bowed woman, with round, red cheeks and wispy grey hair pulled back into a tight little bun on a neck criss-crossed with wrinkles. As she bent over Hammond, she would make odd, inarticulate crooning noises or mutter 'There, there, there!' Clearly her memory was failing. When we encountered each other by chance, she would peer at me with a vague alarm as though wondering who this intruder might be. Her chief occupation was to listen to the war news on the wireless. An arthritic hand cupped round an ear, she would lean towards the over-amplified set in the cramped nook that everyone called 'The wireless room'. Its blackout curtains were frequently left closed, with only a dim overhead light illuminating her tiny form. Lady Hammond never entered there. Now that her cherished son had been so decisively removed from the hostilities, she had lost all interest in them. From time to time Nanny would excitedly come up with the news of some battle won or some city bombed. But as far as Lady Hammond was concerned it might have been the bailiff giving a report on the birth of a calf or the state of the milk yield. Hour after hour her tall, narrow figure would sit upright in a straight-backed chair at a card-table, a game of patience spread out before her. She would stare down, deliberating. Then slowly she would extend a hand, withdraw it, extend it again. Once, as I entered the room with a message from Hammond, she peered up at me with a look of vague distraction. Then she leaned over and moved a card. 'Yes?' I passed on the message. She nodded. No more. Then she said in a fretful voice: 'I'm having no luck with Miss Milligan today. So I'm going to try Sevens.' All her life, I decided, had now become this endlessly extended game of patience.

At weekends, Sir Lionel would appear. He would arrive by train at Manningtree station, seven miles away, and Lady Hammond would drive over to fetch him in the long, sleek Armstrong Siddely that I would sometimes be asked to 'be an angel and polish'. They received a special petrol allowance, partly because of Hammond's disability but chiefly because Sir Lionel was now a junior minister in the Air Ministry. Much of the weekend Sir Lionel would spend in his study, official papers piled up before him. Twice during my time at the Hall, he returned to London immediately after breakfast on the Sunday, after an urgent telephone call from Downing Street. He did not at all care for it when his wife despatched me to summon him to meals. Without a word of thanks, he would explode 'Oh, blast! Oh, hell! Am I never be to left in peace?' An amateur boxer in his youth, he had a large saddle nose, obviously smashed by a fist, its tip a shiny, red pommel. He was constantly raising a forefinger to it and sniffing. He rarely addressed me, and when he did so his tone was always perfunctory, sometimes even contemptuous. It was he who paid me each Saturday, slowly counting out the notes in front of me and then, having handed them over, adding 'You'd better check there's been no mistake.'

From time to time he would travel down with a muscular man with a low, wide forehead, a large nose and hairy forearms. His complexion was so dark and his hair so wiry and black that he might easily have been mistaken for a Greek or an Arab. Whereas I never came to call Hammond by anything other than his surname, Fred was never, at his own insistence, anything other than Fred to me from our first encounter. He had, I soon learned, been Hammond's closest friend in Fighter Command. Miraculously, unlike Hammond, he had survived numerous perilous sorties, which had earned him a DFC – a medal that Hammond had also been awarded. He had then been shifted to a desk job at the Air Ministry. The strength of his attachment to Hammond was immediately clear to me. From time to time, I used to catch him staring, elbows on the arms of his chair and fingers raised in a steeple, at his friend. His eyes squinted with a dazed, frightened distraction, as though he were pondering some life-or-death problem way beyond his intellectual capacities to solve.

On the afternoon of the first of his visits, I was practising at the Bechstein when I became aware that someone had opened the music-room door and was standing motionless on the threshold. I broke off and turned my head.

Fred smiled. '*Le Tombeau de Couperin*? Bravo. Very difficult.' Then he added something that puzzled me at the time. 'Very apt.' Later, sleepless in bed, I wondered about that word 'apt'. Was this an oblique acknowledgement that his friend was doomed, whatever the brave, reassuring things Lady Hammond and 'they' might say?

'You recognised it! Then I can't have been playing so badly.'

He approached the piano. 'That piano's terribly out of tune. The whole family's totally unmusical. I must have a word with Lady H. about getting in a tuner.' Clearly he was on sufficiently close terms with her to make a suggestion that I should never have dared to make.

'Do you play?'

He laughed. 'Well, hardly! I've never had a lesson. But from time to time I vamp something from ear. That's the best that I can do.'

That same evening in the drawing-room after dinner – Sir Lionel had already retired, with a cup of coffee and a cigar to his study – Fred urged me: 'Why don't you play something for us?'

I shook my head.

'Oh, go on!'

'Yes, play something, Mouse. Play, play, play! It may help to pass yet another dreary evening.'

I got up reluctantly and crossed to the piano. Unlike the Bechstein, it was an upright. In addition to the Ravel, I had also been learning the Bach D major Partita. I hesitated about whether to play the Aubade, surely one of the most beautiful pieces of keyboard music ever written, and then, having decided that its resigned melancholy was wrong for the occasion, opted instead for the perky, forward-thrusting Courante.

I had been playing for little more than a minute or two when Hammond shouted: 'Oh, stop, stop, stop! Oh, Mouse! That sounds like a room full of sewing machines going at it hammer and tongs! I can't stand that din.' Mortified, I swung round on the piano stool, preparatory to quitting it. 'Let Fred play something. Come on Fred!'

Fred was reluctant. 'But he was playing that Bach so well. It's far from easy, you know. I'm just an amateur.'

'Oh, come on, Fred!'

I rose from the stool and Fred seated himself at it. There was a pause, as he thought what to play. Then, shoulders and head lowered, he began to toy around with the melody of Gershwin's 'Summertime'. Despite some miscalculations and fumblings, with an occasional 'Blast!' or 'Hell!, he did remarkably well. Lady Hammond had paused in her game of patience. She was staring across the room at the piano, with a look of puzzled, surprised revelation.

'Bravo!' Hammond brought his claw-hands together in an attempt at applause. There was no sound. 'Now how about "Red Sails in the Sunset"?

That was one of your triumphs at the Blue Bear. Remember? At our sing-alongs?'

Fred nodded, mouth pursed. 'All right,' he agreed reluctantly.

'Happy memories.'

I watched from my bedroom window as the woman's bicycle, its high handlebars supporting a wicker basket, zigzagged and wobbled up the drive. The grey-haired, elderly man riding it had no clips on the wide trousers of his faded blue pinstriped suit, so that their ends flapped around his ankles.

'Oh, Mr Friedmann, this is my son's companion.' She did not mention either my real name or that awful 'Mouse' that all of them, with the exception of Fred, still insisted on calling me. 'He's the pianist among us. The piano sounds all right to me but he says it's out of tune.' In fact, I had never said anything to her about the piano being out of tune. It was Fred who had done so.

Friedmann cleared his throat and stooped over the Bechstein. His hands were bluish, with prominent veins. One usually sees elderly people with such hands in the winter, not on a hot summer's day. I noticed, for the first time, the stiff collar with the rounded ends and the small, hard knot of a dark blue tie fraying at the edges. He played a chord, another chord, an arpeggio.

'He is right, my lady. Your piano is out of tune.'

She pulled a little face. 'Well, you know best,' she said.

I left the room with her and then, because I had nothing better to do, soon returned to it. Friedmann was at his work. For much of the time I merely watched him and listened to him. But occasionally he broke off and we talked. He had been released from internment on the Isle of Man only a few months before, he confided in me. Well, better internment there, he added with a sardonic smile, than in a concentration camp. He had been drawn to this part of the world partly because he knew an English couple, owners of a restaurant in Manningtree, who had offered him a room in their house, and partly because of all English painters Constable was the one whom he had always admired the most and Manningtree was so near to Constable's Flatford.

Had he bicycled all the way from Manningtree?

Yes, all the way. He loved the English countryside. It was no hardship to him to bicycle so far. He often bicycled for the fun of it.

He had a soft, hesitant voice, and nervously he kept clearing his throat, raising a small hand to his mouth each time that he did so. There was something both maidenly and steely about him.

Florrie, a maid almost as ancient as Nanny, was banging on the gong. I was going to ignore it but Friedmann said 'They're calling you,.' After a moment of hesitation, I jumped to my feet.

In the doorway I met Lady Hammond.

'Oh, Mr Friedmann, I thought that you might like something to eat before embarking for home. I've asked for a tray to be brought to you.'

'That's really not necessary, my lady.'

'Of course, it's necessary. You have that long ride ahead of you. You don't want to do it on an empty stomach.'

'You are very kind. I thank you.'

She walked to the door, then turned. 'I'll settle with you before you go.'

'Thank you, my lady.'

'Come along, Mouse! The rabbit stew will be getting cold.'

As I sat down to the rabbit – a dish I had come particularly to dislike, since it appeared so often on the menu at the Hall – I suddenly thought how mean-spirited it had been not to invite Friedmann to join us. I almost announced that I hoped that everyone would excuse me if I went to eat with him. Even today, I still feel guilty that I did not have the guts to do so.

The next day, Lady Hammond said to me: 'Oh, Mouse, I'd so much like to meet your mother. When you're next in touch with her, do ask her to come and spend a weekend. She could come on the same train that my husband takes, so there'd be no problem about meeting her.'

I did nothing about the suggestion.

A few days later, when she asked if I had passed on her invitation, I lied with a glibness that surprised me. My mother, I said, had no one with whom to leave the dog, and long journeys with him on a train were always a problem, now that he was so old and, as I put it, liable to make messes.

I had dreaded – absurdly and unjustly, I have long since realised – that if my mother were to accept the invitation, she might be condemned to solitary eating off a tray, just as poor Friedmann had been.

Despite the gloom that enveloped not merely the vast house, most of its rooms now closed for lack of staff, but also the spirits of everyone imprisoned there, in recollection after more than half-a-century it seems as if day after day the sun never ceased to shine. I see it glinting in jagged flashes off the pond, seething with carp. I see it pouring its radiance over the fields as I look down on them from the edge of a dense, strangely sinister little spinney, mysteriously never haunted by birds. I see it making incandescent the panes of the summerhouse, a Gothic folly raised by a prodigal eighteenth century ancestor, who all but ruined the family.

For the rite of the annual cricket match between the village and a neighbouring and rival one, the sun also shone.

After I had inexpertly shaved – 'Oh, for Christ's sake, you've nicked me!' – and dressed Hammond for that occasion, he stared down at his hands. 'Oh, look at my nails. I must do something about them. Sorry, Mouse, you'll have do it for me.' He himself was incapable of properly manipulating the scissors. 'Do you mind awfully?'

'Of course not.' But I did mind. Naturally squeamish, I often minded the tasks that Nanny never minded. Of all those tasks, having to manicure Hammond's hands was, oddly, far more unpleasant for me than having to attend to his bodily functions. As those gristly talons rested on my palm, I was conscious of minuscule grey flakes of skin falling off them like ash. The task done, I had to find some excuse to leave the room and first brush myself down with panicky movements of my hands and then hurry into the cloakroom, where I soaped and scrubbed them.

'How did these nails get so long? It can't be more than a week since you last did them.' He looked up at me. 'Did you know that nails continue to grow on a corpse.' He smiled. 'True.'

I nodded. Having reached for the file on the table beside me, I smoothed a rough edge. Then, suddenly and surprisingly, I felt an annihilating tenderness that I had never felt before when doing his nails. I looked down at the cruelly distorted hands and then up into the even more cruelly distorted face. I felt an ache in my throat, as though some indissoluble object had lodged there, and a sudden fullness of the eyes.

Since his disability had made him hypersensitive to other people's feelings and thoughts, whereas in the past he had been entirely indifferent to them, he must, I now realise, have intuited my feelings. When I had finished the job, he said 'Thank you' in a barely audible voice, using not the hated 'Mouse' but (something that rarely happened) my Christian name. 'What would I do without you?'

'Oh, I'm sure you'd manage very well.'

14

Fred and I took it in turns to wheel the chair to the cricket ground, beyond the church. Fred propelled it effortlessly along the narrow up-and-down path, as though it were no more than a pushchair with a baby in it. I struggled at every bump and twist and soon began to wheeze and sweat. Eventually, with none of his usual contempt and impatience when I showed my ineptitude, Hammond said quietly: 'You'd better give up, Mouse. Let Fred do it. We don't want your asthma to ruin the day for you.'

'No, no, I can manage. Really.'

But Fred was already moving into position, edging me aside.

I had hated cricket at school, not merely because I was so hopeless at it but also because it proceeded so slowly and interminably. But all that day, as Fred and I sat out on the grass beside Hammond in his wheelchair and his parents reclined in deck-chairs brought out to them by one of the organisers of the match, the local butcher, I felt inexplicably happy. From time to time I would look up at Hammond, as he stared out eagerly at all the activity − or, as I saw it, dearth of activity − on the field before us. At school, he had been the captain and hero of the First XI, just as he had been an athlete often tipped to be the first man to achieve a four-minute mile. He was keeping up a running commentary: 'Oh, Christ, what a shot! … Idiot! Couldn't he see that that was a googly? … Oh, good, good, good …'

Soon Sir Lionel was pouring out shots of Scotch into silver tumblers that fitted into each other like Russian dolls. When, finally, he came to one for me, I shook my head. 'Not for me. Thank you.'

He scowled at me. 'Oh, come on! Be a man!'

I again shook my head. I took pleasure in defying him.

'Well, please yourself. Perhaps Lady Hammond can spare you some of her coffee.'

Shortly before the lunch interval, Hammond asked me to wheel him to the lavatory behind the pavilion. As the chair bumped from tussock to tussock, he said: 'You poor chap! I ought to have asked Fred to take me. But by now you know the drill and he doesn't.' The 'drill' had always repelled me. But, amazingly, for once it did not now do so.

As I took the bottle from him − when he went out, it always went with him in a canvas bag − he pointed: 'Is that blood?'

I peered in horror. Through the glass, what looked like lengths of scarlet thread were gently wavering in the orange urine.

'Oh God, don't say I've started the bleeding again!'

I had never known him to bleed while I had been with him.

'Do you want to go home?'

'No. Of course not! Don't be such an ass. But it's' – he smiled up at me – 'inconvenient.'

For the rest of the day he was more cheerful than I had ever known him. After the match was over, I wheeled him from one group of people to another. Since he was not merely the son of the squire but also the local hero, there was a certain obsequiousness in everyone's behaviour to him. At the high tea that followed back at the Hall, he made a speech that, unlike his father's portentous one, was exactly right for the occasion in its judicious blend of humour, self-deprecation and love for the village in which his family had lived for so many centuries. I realised that he could easily have followed his father into politics.

'Well, that was a good day, Mouse,' he said, as I put my hand to the switch of the overhead light, before leaving him, propped up on three pillows, on his orthopaedic bed. I slept in the next-door dressing-room – always lightly, so as to be ready for his summons.

'Yes. Wonderful.'

'But cricket's not quite your thing, is it?'

'That's true. But – but – yes, it was wonderful. A wonderful day.'

Nanny and I sat facing each other in the middle of the table that seemed to stretch endlessly away in the light from two forty-watt bulbs. In those years to save electricity, as to save everything thing else, had become a patriotic duty. Neither of us had had any appetite for what Lady Hammond had referred to as 'cold cuts' – thin greasy slices of ham and shiny chicken interleaved with each other, purple on white. She had driven to Manningtree to meet the last train from London. For once Sir Lionel was coming back to the Hall on a weekday, bringing with him the famous specialist, now an octogenarian, who had come out of retirement because of the war. Hammond was asleep upstairs. He now had two nurses, both stout, elderly woman in white starched uniforms, to nurse him round the clock.

Nanny munched, looking not at me but sideways and over her shoulder as though in a dealer's appraisal of the boulle cabinet under the window to her left. As so often when we were alone together, there had been a long but not uncomfortable silence between us. I had been lost in thoughts of Hammond. Perhaps she had too. Certainly it was of him that she now began to talk, with her slight West Country burr. 'It's the kidneys. That's the trouble. They were crushed, you know. Kidneys can't grow again. And you can't replace them, can you? If they're not working properly, then the system is poisoned.' She put down her knife and fork and then raised her napkin to her lips. 'He was such a strong little boy. Never ill. And he never cried. Never. Even after he had had a fall into the empty swimming-pool he never cried. We thought then that he might have broken a leg, but it was only a bruising.' Her mistily pale blue eyes, with their inflamed upper lids, stared at me, as though trying to sum me up.

'Do you think this specialist can do something?' I think that I already knew the answer to that question: no.

'Well, dear, we must go on believing that he can. Mustn't we? We have to have that faith. If we believe enough ...' A Roman Catholic, she would each Sunday walk three miles across the fields to the nearest Roman Catholic church and then walk back again. Once I said to her: 'Couldn't you bicycle?,' to receive the firm answer 'No, I couldn't do with that.'

I, too, now put down my knife and fork.

'Maureen has left an apple tart.' She got to her feet and peered. 'And some custard by the look of it. Too thin, as always. How about that?'

'Thank you, no. I don't feel all that hungry.'

She sat down again.

'Wouldn't you like some?'

She shook her head. 'I'm not a great one for puddings,' she said, as she had often said before. She raised her tumbler of water and sipped at it, then sipped again. 'Wars are terrible things.'

'Well, yes, they are.'

'My fiancé was killed in the war, you know. Did I ever tell you that? I mean the war before this one.' How could I have supposed that she might mean the present one? 'At Mons. You may have heard of Mons. Thousands and thousands of people were killed there, you know. English, French, Huns. And he was one of them. Later, people – meaning to be kind of course – used to tell me that someone else would come along for me. That's what they used to tell me. Someone else. But there was no one else. How could there be? After the war, there were too many women for the men to go around. So here I am.' She raised her glass and sipped again. 'But it's not been a bad life. I've been lucky to have spent all these years here. The house is almost a palace, isn't it? And Mr Derek has been like a son to me. His mother was always so busy, you know. In those days, when he was growing up. She had all those charities and she loved her hunting. And – oh – all those other things.' She squinted at me, her mouth pursed, and then said in a suddenly sharp voice: 'It's odd, your not having been called up.'

'I'm exempt. I have asthma.' There was no reason why I should feel self-defensive and guilty but I did.

'Oh, yes, your asthma!'

A silence followed, eventually broken by the sound of voices from beyond the dining-room door.

Nanny jumped to her feet. 'Oh, there they are!'

I soon came to hate the rigid manner of the two nurses in their starchy uniforms. Clearly, they resented my intrusions into the sickroom. Clearly too, they even more resented any task that Hammond asked me to do for him. On one occasion, as I was patting a pillow, one of the two women snatched it from me. 'I can do that!' A few days later, when I had begun to read to him the news from the *Morning Post*, the other, who was then on duty, interrupted: 'I think he ought to get some sleep now. Doctor said that sleep was the best thing for him.' No longer did I occupy the dressing-room, since that was where, the door always open, one or other was always sentinel. My new room, far larger, with a yellowing sitz-bath with rusty taps in one corner of it, was at the other end of the long corridor.

One afternoon, when one of the two had left and the other had still not arrived, I was alone with Hammond. His face was blotched with curious reddish-purple swellings, each the size of a then penny piece, and his forehead was creased and shiny with sweat. His eyes were closed as, seated in an upright chair, I stared across at him with a dull, heavy mingling of repugnance and grief. There was a rusty stain of blood, shaped like a star, on his pillow, whether from his mouth, his nose or somewhere else I could only guess. The ammoniac smell was overpowering.

His eyes opened blearily. He stared, then screwed them up. 'Mouse,' he muttered.

'Mouse. Oh, Mouse. It's you.'

I got up slowly, approached the bed and lowered my hand. At once, with a swiftness that struck me with momentary terror, one of the claw-hands shot up and gripped it. 'Oh, Mouse, I feel so ill. Why do I feel so ill?'

'It's because of the temperature. That's all. But it's going down,' I added, lying. 'You're getting better.'

'Oh, don't be silly, Mouse. I've had it. I'm sure I've had it. I thought I'd had it after the crash and I was wrong. But this time …' He raised his head and then let it fall back sideways on the pillow.

'I forgot to shave you this morning.' I had noticed, for the first time, the stubble on his chin. He was always so careful about his appearance.

'Did you know that the hair and the nails still grow on dead people?' The almost exact repetition of what he had once before said to me was eerie.

Once again the claw-hand shot out and grabbed mine. The astonishing strength of its grip almost made me cry out. I remember thinking: a drowning man might grip one like that.

'You know, Mouse, I'm frightened. Terrified. Yes, terrified.' His body jerked from side to side as though in an epileptic spasm. Then suddenly he yelped: 'Oh, hold me, Mouse, hold me! I'm losing everything!'

I had always tried to touch him as little as possible. I had always hated doing all those intimate things that had become part of my daily duties until the arrival of the nurses. But now I leaned over the bed and put my arms around him. His body shuddered against mine. Then he began to sob, in what sounded like a prolonged, useless bout of retching.

The door opened. The resonant, contralto voice of the larger of the nurses said: 'Now how are things in here?'

I at once let go of him and scrambled to my feet.

'I must change that pillow case. And give him his injection.'

She was telling me to go.

I was with him only once again. It was on the eve of my departure. He wanted to see me, Lady Hammond said, interrupting me as I was yet again playing the Bach Aubade. In those days I never ceased to find in it the solace that Nanny clearly found in her daily trudges to the church. Lady Hammond was haggard, her lower eyelids sagging strangely so that the eyes looked much larger than usual, and her voice rasped. 'Don't stay too long with him. He's terribly weak. Just say goodbye. Just that. That's all.'

The two nurses were eating together in the next-door dressing room. They had turned on the wireless that Lady Hammond had provided for them but were talking animatedly and from time to time laughing above the voice, measured and grave, reading the news. There was an occasional clink of cutlery on crockery.

His eyes were shut. I did not know whether to say something or leave him. I stared down. I had always felt him to be so much larger than I was. Now the thought came: How small he is. There came another thought: He's like a mouse. A dead mouse. Crushed in a trap from which there's no escape.

He stirred. He opened his eyes, which were rimmed with something sticky and yellow. Was it pus? For a while he stared up at me and then he smiled. 'Mouse,' he whispered. 'Good old mouse.' He brought out a claw-hand from under the sheet and held it out to me.

I took it. 'I'm leaving tomorrow. Early. Your mother's going to drive me to the station with your father. I've come to say goodbye. And thank you.'

'Oh, Mouse, are you going? I hadn't realised. Why didn't you tell me?'

In fact I had told him. He couldn't have taken it in. 'Term. Term starts. I have to go.'

'But what'll I do without you?' It was not the usual question, asked merely as a convention of regret. I knew, with a pang of sorrow and guilt, that he really meant it. On an impulse I said: 'I'll stay if you like. Would you like that? Yes, please let me stay.'

Violently he shook his head from side to side on the pillow. 'No, no! I wouldn't dream of it. You mustn't be late for term. Don't feel you have to stick with me to the end. Don't feel you have to do that. No. You must go, Mouse. You must get on with it. Become another Rubinstein. Or another Solomon. No time to be lost! You must get on with it!'

I edged away from the bed. But I still stared down at him. Then I made up my mind: 'But I'd like to stay on. Truly. Term doesn't matter all that much. I can make some excuse. I can say that I'm ill – or that my mother is ill – or that our flat has been bombed. Something like that. Easy. Oh, let me stay!'

He might not have heard me. 'Oh, there's something I want you to have. For all you've done for me. It's – it's over there, I think. Nothing much. In the left-side drawer. Top. Over there.' He pointed at the chest-of-drawers under the window. 'It's my DFC. Take it. Keep it. Go on! It's no bloody use to me. A souvenir for you of a thoroughly boring summer.'

'Oh, no. No! I couldn't do that. Your mother and father ... They must have it. They'd want it. It wouldn't be right. No.'

Suddenly, shamefully, I felt the tears welling from my eyes.

'Oh, very well. If that's how you feel! Anyway, thank you – thank you, Mouse. Thank you for helping through all this.' He peered up at me. 'Mouse. *Mouse!* You're not blubbing, are you? Oh, for Christ's sake!' His voice had weirdly changed. It now had the tone, jocular and yet vaguely jeering, of those now remote days when I had been a mouse to his lion. 'Stop it, Mouse! Oh, stop it! Don't be such a bloody fool! *Stop it!* What's the matter with you?'

I turned away. As I did so, I noticed that one of the letters that I used sporadically to answer for him had blown off the desk under the open window on to the carpet. I stooped, picked it up and returned it to the pile. After that, I walked on to the door and, without looking round, left him for the last time.

The Pushchair

These days he feels either moribund, staring down dejectedly at a book that he hardly takes in or at *The Times* crossword that he can now rarely finish, or else twitchingly restless, as a knee jerks, his knuckles creak as he cracks them, or he keeps biting his dry lips, sometimes making them ooze a small, lethargic bead of blood. Having left the bags of shopping on the kitchen table, he sits for a few minutes staring at them, but then totters up and begins to wander about the capacious Edwardian house, pausing from time to time to stare at some picture or object that will soon be carted away for the sale. *These fragments have I shored against my ruin.* But the fragments are valuable, so Elsie constantly reminds him. You won't want for a bob or two, is how she puts it.

He stares out of his study window. A listless snow is drifting down on the overgrown garden, flake by flake. The blackbird – there are, in fact, a number of blackbirds but he never sees more than one at a time and so thinks there is only one – is up there hunched on a branch of the hawthorn. Poor chap. *It's only in December that birds ever look dejected. Perhaps they too suffer from SAD, like myself.*

He begins effortfully to mount the stairs, half-dragging himself with a hand clutching at the banister. He has no purpose at the top – or, if he did, he has already forgotten it. Elsie must have omitted to shut the door to the flight of narrow steps that now beckon him on, up, up to the attic. No wonder the house feels so icy. She spent yesterday afternoon sorting things. *No, I don't need your help, father. You'll only make your bronchitis worse in the cold up here. Please!* He obeyed her, as he always did. But for some reason he felt an all but physical nausea at the thought of those stubby-fingered, capable hands violating the debris of both his life and that of her mother, dead these fourteen – no, now fifteen – years.

The smell that, surrounded by dusty, broken pieces of furniture, suitcases and packing cases, he now begins to inhale, strikes him, weirdly, as not an indoor but an outdoor one. He thinks of a damp nook of the garden, bare, black boughs above him and a rank mulch of leaves at his feet. The image makes him shiver, crooked fingers pressed to mouth. *Oh, drat the girl!* But she is no longer a girl but a woman of fifty-four. *Why did she have to leave those copies of the* Studio *scattered everywhere? What was she doing with them?* For the last, oh, how many years he had carefully stored every issue there, in a neat row of packing cases. Now – total disorder! A whole set like that is valuable, for heaven's sake.

He touches a jumbo arm-chair slumped in a corner, trails a hand over a rickety towel-rail, and then peers into a cabin trunk, the open lid of which reveals some swathes of cretonne eventually recognised as having once been the curtains of the bedroom that he shared with his wife for all those uneventful, happy years. There used to be a light switch somewhere hereabouts. Yes, yes. He touches it, eases the switch upwards. Funny, he has remembered that, upwards, not downwards. Head lowered, to avoid the increasing slope of the roof, he totters on, pausing to peer, in the low-wattage light, now at this dusty object, now at that. Is it tomorrow that *they*, whoever they are, are coming to cart away all of these things except those that have been earmarked by Elsie and the man from Sotheby's?

Suddenly, in the farthest corner, leaning against the huge water-tank, he sees it: the pushchair. How did that get there? Like the glimpse of some apparition or the discovery of a corpse, it transmits an instant buzz of terror. He zigzags over to it. Beside it there is a wicker basket, of the kind used to transport an ailing cat to the vet, a pale-blue suitcase, one hasp of which hangs broken, and four or five plastic bags all but bursting with clothes. The pushchair and all the other things are festooned with spider-webs. He picks up one of the plastic bags, peers into it, and jerks out something knitted in red and blue wool. It's a child's – what? – jumper? He puts the jumper to his cheek, then abruptly drops it to the floor, as though it were burning his fingers. He drags the pushchair towards him. *She's pushing it – or am I pushing it? – and we're both laughing, and he, she, the child is laughing, turning his (yes, yes, a boy, Ivor, Ivan, something like that) turning his head up and around to look at us.* The thorn-like memory jabs at him.

Later, after he has microwaved for his supper the spaghetti bolognese left by Elsie in the deep freeze, he sits by the empty fireplace in the sitting-room overheated by three radiators, and broods for a while, as he often now does, on the future ahead of him. *Melanie and I would so much like to have offered you a refuge. We feel guilty about it. But, as you know, there are only those two bedrooms and in any case we're both out all day and often late into the evening. Everyone says that that home is one of the best in the country.* That was reasonable enough. He could never have fitted in with them in that small space. But his resentment against the woman usurper of the attention that he still feels, in a reversal of the usual parent-child relationship, should be his exclusively, has only intensified. *You've robbed me of my daughter. You've robbed me of her love.*

As though to escape from tasting the poisonous bitterness of that rejection, he once more thinks of the pushchair. An image comes to him: his hand and the girl's hand, resting side by side, pushing it simultaneously. *Am I imagining it? Or did that really happen?* She was so fragile-looking and yet was so strong. It was the same with her hands. Small hands, but with a strength that always amazed him. *I can't get this wretched jar open.* A quick twist by those small hands to the lid and he could then scoop out his marmalade. *Thanks! Thanks! Terrific!*

It was through Elsie that she and the child had come to him. *Now that mother's no longer with you and I'm so rarely home, you need someone. You're not used to looking after yourself. One hears of confirmed bachelors. You're a confirmed widower. Yes, you really need someone.* He wanted to say: *It's you I need. Only you.* But they never said things as dramatic and self-revelatory as that to each other. *You'd also be doing her a good turn. The poor thing is desperate.*

Lidia (yes, the second letter an 'i', not a 'y' as he had at first supposed) was a Hungarian. She and her husband, a dark-skinned Brazilian waiter in a Pall Mall club, lived with their infant son in the flat next to Elsie's. That was long before Elsie and Melanie had met and had moved into a mansion flat of their own overlooking Holland Park. This was a poky one, rented not bought, in Hackney. The couple were constantly fighting, with doors reverberantly slamming and voices exploding upwards, in jagged splinters, from the dank well. Elsie at first complained, something for which she had a talent, and then comforted, something for which she had less of one. Would she have done the second of those things if the young mother had not been so appealing in her woebegone fragility?

The man's clearly a brute. I can't imagine what she sees in him.

He smiled slyly. *Perhaps he's wonderful in bed?*

Elsie pulled a face. She didn't care for the idea of that.

There were feeble excuses for the bruises and lacerations – a trip over a carpet, a kitchen cupboard door inadvertently left open. Then, one night, there was the hammering on the door – *Please, please let me in!* – and Elsie in pyjamas was confronting the couple, the girl with the baby tucked in the crook of an arm and that brute gripping her shoulder and shouting 'Come back! Come in!' With a hiccup of a sob the girl suddenly obeyed him. As she did so, the baby, previously so silent that he might have been dead, began to wail. Elsie shouted at their retreating backs: 'I'll call the police if there's any more of this!'

It was when the Brazilian, a fanatical supporter of Arsenal, was away in Belgium for two days to attend a match, that Elsie hatched her plot. *It's the perfect solution for you, father. She worked as an au pair for some lawyer and his wife in Hampstead. She's a sweet child. And the baby won't be any trouble if you put them in the basement flat. You need someone like that. And you'll be doing her a good turn.* She had difficulty in persuading him; but, as so often in the past, her tenacity eventually overcame his reluctance.

He had never cared for young children. But he had had to admit that the baby was no trouble at all. Lidia never let him out of her sight, as she energetically pushed and dragged the antiquated Hoover around room after room, made the vast double bed in one corner of which he would sleep late into the morning, or prepared one of her delicious Madeira cakes. At dinner parties, she would often be carrying the child on her back as she steered her way around the table. 'Are you offering me a choice between the potatoes and your baby?' one guest once jokingly asked.

That combination of sweetness and strength. It's irresistible. I'm so glad that you thought of the idea. It's the best thing that's happened to me since your poor mother died.

He never felt closer than when he and Lidia would venture out together with the pushchair. *I really must buy you a new one.* But she was always careful even with money not hers. *Oh, no. It's fine. Fine.* She had bought it from another of her London neighbours, whose child had outgrown it. He would feel suddenly light-headed and, yes, inexplicably happy, as he helped her lift the pushchair up the steps or stood with it on the sea-front, smiling down alternately at the child and at the gentle, sunlit waves, as she scuttled across the road, short-cropped blonde hair glistening, to buy him his evening paper. *Oh, no, no!* He could still hear her protesting, so many years after she had vanished from his life, against his purchase of yet another present for the child. *You spoil him.* So far from spoiling Elsie, he had always been strict with her.

Strangely, when he had opened the door and seen the tall, dark, narrow-faced man standing before him, he knew at once who he was.

Lidia is here. A statement, not a question.

Who are you? Why do you want to see her?

Then there she was, standing behind him, the child, as so often, in a crook of her arm. *It's all right. It's fine.*

But he could not believe that it was all right, fine. Reluctantly he moved aside. Why, *why?* Why had he failed to stand his ground? He was often to ask himself that question.

We are going little walk together.

He gripped the cretonne curtain in one hand and gazed down to the steep street. The man did not help her with the pushchair, as he himself would have done, but merely stood watching her as she struggled to manhandle it down the steps. But he took over from her as soon as she had eased it through the gate. He then began to push it down the hill towards the sea. Oddly, Lidia walked not beside him but behind him. For a moment she halted and looked up at the window and the old man could see – or thought he could see – the beseeching terror and anguish on her face.

But when they at last returned – all through their absence he had kept his frozen vigil at the window – the two of them were pushing the chair together, just as he and she had so often pushed it together in the past, their hands often touching, and she was talking, smiling, laughing, as was the tall, dark, narrow-faced man.

I'm sorry. Very sorry. But I think it best if we go back with my husband.

Oh, do you really think so? Are you sure?

I think it best.

But not now, not at once!

Better. Yes. I'm sorry. You are so kind, always so kind.

They would be taking the train. Might they leave the pushchair and some other things until they could return in a day or two? Her husband would borrow a van from a friend of his.

Well, yes, of course. If that's what you want. Of course.

He never saw them again. He never heard from them again. Elsie said that they had vanished from the flat two or three days after their return to it. She made enquiries of the landlords, of the other tenants, and of the Pakistani owner of the store at the corner. But no one had any information. Perhaps they had moved to Brazil. Perhaps to Hungary. Those were the usual surmises.

But it's so odd!

Yes, it is odd. I hope the poor thing and the baby are all right.

Elsie eventually told him that she had spoken to the police. But they had been 'unhelpful'.

I was unhelpful too. I should have done something. He thought that but did not say it.

A ferocious gale battered the seaside town all that night. By turns he slept, half-slept, and lay awake. *What am I doing in this tiny boat without any oars? It's dark and what ought to be water when a wave crashes over me is not water but blood. I feel sick. Seasick, life-sick. Will no one rescue me?* That was one dream. He awoke from it to reach out for the glass of water by his bedstead and gulp from it. His throat and mouth felt parched. Then, soon after, still awake, he had to urinate. He remembered, with a terrible pang, how Lidia would leave a glass of water by the vast bed every evening and how she would each morning empty the chamber-pot and scour it out with something that made it stink no longer of urine but, even less agreeably, of carbolic. *Why is that it is only in works of fiction and in accounts given by patients to psychiatrists do dreams have a coherent, consequential logic, however perverse?*

Once more he drops off, as over a cliff into a boiling sea. *Whose room is this that I'm about to enter? Oh, it's the attic! And why am I so terrified of turning the doorknob? But I must, must, must. The light switch. I can't see a thing. Yes, up, not down. I remember that. The sudden glare from the overhead bulb – or is it the sudden terror that I feel? – makes me close my eyes tight shut. Open them, must, must. Blood glistens everywhere. It makes zigzag patterns on the walls and the carpet. It drips off the chimneypiece and the vast, dangling light-bulb. The room is empty. No one, nothing there. Except, yes, in the centre of it, yes, the pushchair. Smashed, crushed. It might have been run over by a lorry or a train.*

He woke, sat up in the bed, and then scrabbled out of it, frenziedly pushing away the bedclothes as though they too were soaked in blood. *That man, with his dark, stern, narrow face, must have killed them both. Must have. He did. Why did I never realise? Why? Why?*

Over breakfast he mused on the dream, as he sipped at an acrid cup of instant coffee made, as always, with two teaspoons, not one, from the jar. Yesterday, on his visit to Safeway, he had forgotten to buy any bread and so he had had to toast a stale crust originally intended for the birds. He now constantly dreamed, so that his sleeping life had long since become far more filled with incident than his waking one. He was convinced that through those confused, often terrible night-time visions a voice — perhaps the voice of the person that he once was, perhaps the voice of the person that he was still to become, perhaps even the voice of some guardian angel or even devil — was trying to make itself intelligible to him. *Yes, that brute must have killed them both.* He nodded to himself, cup to lips, with a lurching, giddying sensation of mingled horror and grief.

Later, in a crescendo of dread, he once again mounted the stairs to the attic. He half expected to find it as in his dream — splashed with blood, empty but for the pushchair, the pushchair smashed. But it was all as it always was: dimly lit by a single forty-watt bulb, dusty, crowded with the debris of times long gone.

He was breathless from the ascent and his legs were trembling. He sank down on to an old cabin trunk, so heavy that it had ceased to be used when porters had ceased to exist, and gasped for air. He put out a hand to the handle of the pushchair and let it rest there. Then, slowly, he began to push it back and forth, back and forth, as he used to do when he and the child were waiting for Lidia's return. It squeaked and it creaked, the two sounds alternating at regular intervals. It was that regularity that eventually brought him first consolation and then an overwhelming sense of both fatigue and repose. His eyes closed. The hand ceased to push and pull. The pushchair was stationary and silent.

The Interrogations

He had been lively on the first day. He had asked me to prop him up on the pillows – 'No, no! She can do it' he irritably told the black nurse, who had just taken his temperature and blood pressure and was about to start on the pillows. 'Let my daughter do it. She's strong. She's got plenty of time and you've made it clear that you've far too much on your hands already.'

With a sigh and a frown, the nurse left the room.

'She's always in a hurry, that one. All the nurses here are in a hurry. All of them seem to be either black or Australians. I prefer the Australians. I hate it when that woman touches me. I can smell her when she's close. Why do they all have that peculiar smell?'

I was appalled. But, as others so often reminded me and as I so often reminded myself, one had to make allowances for a man of eighty-four. He belonged to a different era, almost to a different species, at once more jovial and more brutal than ours. He had also worked for most of his life as jute-merchant in Bombay, with large domestic and office staffs of Indians, whom he had treated as serfs. Once again I told myself that I mustn't 'lose my rag' – as he would often put it when I lost my temper with him. So all I said, as though making a joke of it, was: 'Oh, father, please! You must get over these prehistoric attitudes of yours.'

'You know by now that I have no use for this political correctness. I say what I think. I've always done so. I'll go on doing so. If that's prehistoric, so be it.'

I decided to change the subject. 'How is it here?'

'Well, you can see for yourself. It's not a bad room. The kind you'd accept in a two-star hotel.' For a while his grating cough silenced him. He swallowed hard, and swallowed again, as though something had stuck in his throat. 'And the staff are all right except – as you saw for yourself – they're always in a hurry.'

'Is the television now working?'

'Yes, a man – another black of course – came to fix it. Channel One is still a fuzz. But otherwise it's fine. Not that I get much pleasure out of it these days. I can't hear it properly, can't see it properly.'

'And the food?'

'Passable. They must keep the microwave busy.'

'Roy sent his best wishes. And the children. They plan to visit you at the weekend.'

'Decent of them.' He was clearly not interested. He was not going to ask whether Roy had had any news about the job for which he was in the running, or whether Janet's worryingly persistent rash was any better.

He licked his dry lips, closed his eyes, grunted, sighed. The shrivelled leaf of his consciousness eddied, dipped, and was sucked down into the still, dark, dangerous waters on which it had been floating.

The silent interrogation began.

Why am I here?

Because we could no longer cope with you.

Wasn't the house large enough?

Yes. Yes, of course.

And who gave you the house?

You did, father. As our wedding present.

Didn't I always love you more than your stepbrother and stepsisters?

Yes. Yes, I believe that.

Then why did you decide to dump me here?

It wasn't a question of dumping you. We did what we thought was best.

Best for me or best for you all?

Best for you and for us.

You said you couldn't cope. But you had the carers. Not that they were much bloody good. But still – you had the carers. Didn't you?

Yes, we had the carers. But they cost money. Four carers in all. A lot of money.

My money?

Yes, but it was running out. Fast.

And you didn't want that, did you?

Mercifully, at that moment the shrivelled leaf slowly resurfaced. He drew a long sigh, his amazingly pale-blue eyes fluttered open, he put a gnarled hand up to his cheek and brushed it, as though to remove an invisible cobweb. The signet ring that my mother gave him on their wedding day glinted in the late sunlight from the window beside the bed. I am now wearing it myself. It has the crest of her family, an old and distinguished one, engraved on it. His family was a prosperous one of builders' merchants, but they had never had a crest. He was proud of my mother's crest.

'I dropped off.' He turned his head from side to side, eyes searching. 'What's happened to my tea?'

'Oh, it's far too early for tea, father.'

'Time goes so slowly here.'

'Would you like one of the Jaffa cakes I brought.'

'No.'

'Or some barley water?'

'No.'

The black nurse was called Beryl and she came from St Kitts. We had little chats, never in his room but when we met fortuitously in the corridor or at the reception desk. 'How is he?' I used to ask. 'I hope he's not being too difficult?' I added once. She replied: 'Well, he's a real character, isn't he?' One afternoon she told me that she was going off early because her son was having a tonsillectomy at the Royal Free. 'NHS,' she added. Was it a dig, an oblique reproach? I decided that, if it were, it was better to ignore it. Instead I asked how many children she had. Six. When I mistakenly told him this, he pulled a face, as though he had unexpectedly tasted something bitter. 'They breed like rabbits.'

He was getting frailer and vaguer. Roy had once remarked, partly in hatred and partly in admiration: 'He has such a sharp edge to him.' Now that edge was increasingly blunt and rusty.

'Would you like me to read to you?'

He shook his head. 'I can't hear you properly. It's the frequency. The high frequency. Your voice is too high for me. I can hear that black creature. Perfectly. Her voice is like a female impersonator's. Not that I want to hear her.'

'What have you been watching on television?'

'Nothing. It's all so dreadful.'

'Don't you watch the sport?' When he lived with us, he would drive Roy crazy with the sound turned up to full as he watched some football match or athletics programme.

'Can't be bothered.' He had been a champion marathon runner just before the War, in which he had served with so much gallantry.

He closed his eyes. 'Well,' he said. Then, more softly, merely a whisper: 'Well.'

The shrivelled leaf was eddying, about to descend once again into the dark and cold.

Roy doesn't like me, does he?

Of course he does.

Don't you remember when he shouted at you in one of his rages: We've just got to get rid of the old bugger?

He didn't mean it. You know what he's like. When he loses his temper he comes out with silly things like that. He doesn't mean them.

Are you happy with him?

Yes. Of course.

Fortunately at that moment Beryl entered the room. 'I must just take his temperature' she said. I wanted to say 'What's the point of constantly taking his temperature? He's dying, isn't he?' Instead I leaned over him and shook his arm. He stirred, opened his eye. He glared at Beryl. Then 'Fuck!' The word was like a rifle shot in an empty room. 'What the hell are you doing here?'

'Sorry. I have to take your temperature.' She approached his bed with a slight waddle, her large breasts jutting out under her white apron. Roy would find her attractive, I thought. Voluptuously ample, totally unlike me, she was his sort of woman. 'What a mess you've got your bed into.' She might have been our Finnish au pair talking to one of the children. 'Let me deal with those pillows.' She put out a strong, fleshy arm, placed it around his shoulders and then eased him up. With the other arm she tweaked the top pillow away from under him.

'Oh, you bitch!' he bawled. 'You did that on purpose. You hurt me on purpose. You know how painful my neck has become.'

'I'm sorry,' she said coldly. She looked across at me, shrugged, pulled a face. 'There's no need to talk me like that.'

'Oh, get out of here. Get out!' He yelled the last two words.

Again the shrug, the pulling of a face. 'And what about your temperature?'

She once more approached the bed and extended the thermometer.

I expected him to shout more abuse at her. Had he bitten the thermometer once she had placed it in his mouth, I should not have been surprised. But now, to my astonishment, he was suddenly docile. Hands to his sides outside the bedclothes, he stared up the ceiling.

'It's a glorious day,' Beryl turned her head to say to me, as she waited for the thermometer to cook.

'How's your son?'

'Oh, he's fine now. His throat's a little sore still. But he's back at school.'

'That's good.'

After she had plucked away the thermometer, examined it and left the room, I demanded: 'How could you speak to her like that. What's the matter with you?'

'What's the matter with me? Haven't you realised? I'm dying.'

'That's no excuse. No excuse at all. If the living owe a duty of respect to the dying, then the dying owe a similar duty of respect to the living. I was utterly ashamed of you.'

'Oh, she's such a useless bitch. And I've told you, I hate that *smell* of hers.'

'What are you talking about? Smell, smell, smell! She has no smell, except the smell of soap. It's your whole attitude that stinks. You seem to think that you're back in India shouting abuse at the wogs. You're not. Whether you like it or not, you're in another world. You've got to learn to behave in it.'

'Oh, it's too late for that. You can't teach a dying dog new tricks.'

He closed his eyes. His usually grey face was blotched with an angry red. He had drifted away from me.

How can you bring yourself to speak to me like that? I thought you loved me.

I do love you, father. But you're driving me crazy. Why can't you die with decency and dignity?

Because dying is such an indecent and undignified thing. Do you now dread your visits to me?

Yes. Yes, I have to say it. Yes, I do. You frighten me. You shock me.

Would you rather not come?

Oh, no. No. I must come.

Every day. Why? I'm lucky if I see your stepbrother and stepsisters once a week. I have a sense of duty. It's an awful nuisance. I inherited it from mother.

Don't you have anything more than that?

Yes.

What?

Well, love, I suppose.

His legs suddenly began to twitch under the bedclothes. Dogs' legs twitch like that when they are dreaming. His eyes opened. He stared at me, as if at a stranger.

'Father!' The cry emerged from somewhere deep inside me with a terrible, tearing sensation. I jumped up and put my hands to his emaciated shoulders, my cold cheek against his hot one. Then I felt his hands pushing me away, with extraordinary violence for someone so ill. 'Come on! Come on! What's got into you?' he protested.

From that visit, his attitude to Beryl wholly changed. He had never before called her by her name. Now he constantly did so, as though just to utter it gave him pleasure. Those bleak, extraordinarily pale blue eyes would suddenly darken and soften as he watched her going about her humdrum tasks of handing him his innumerable pills and then extending a tumbler of water, of taking away a vase of dead flowers or bringing in a vase of fresh ones, of straightening his sheets, of tidying his slippers or the books and magazines on his table. 'Ah, there's Beryl,' he would say when she entered the room. 'Beryl is going to take her children to Alton Towers,' he told me. 'Tomorrow she has the day off. So the children will be the gainers and I'm to be the loser.' 'Beryl has brought me her *Mail*. There's a long article about the ludicrous delays in getting Athens ready for the Olympics.'

She comes into the room and he at once turns his head away from me to look at her. 'Oh, goodness, your pyjama top is soaked!' Now he yields himself gratefully to her ministrations. There is a yearning look in his eyes as she eases off the top and wipes down with a towel the once powerful, now emaciated chest, with the livid scar puckering down it. Curiously, there is the same yearning look in her eyes too. Before, she has carried out her tasks, often unpleasant and always unwelcome, with an unheeding briskness. Now her capable hands seem to linger over each small service with rare delicacy and, yes, tenderness. Those services have become stages in a secret rite that only they share. I am excluded from it. 'That's better,' she says. 'The poor dear is getting these sudden fevers.' She stoops over him. 'Would you like a cup of tea?'

He shakes his head, smiles. The smile irradiates the shrunken face. 'Perhaps for my daughter,' he says.

'Yes, of course, dear.' There was a time near the beginning of his stay when she called him 'dear' and he shouted at her 'I'm not your dear.' Viciously he then added: 'Get that, *dear?*'

'I'm glad you're getting on so much better with her. She's a decent soul – and such a good nurse.'

'Yes, she's a marvel.'

I am amazed.

He is rambling on to me about a holiday that we once took, all of us, to a rented house in the hills above Menton twenty, thirty years ago. 'Do you remember the yacht...?'

'Yes, yes,' I say eagerly.

Suddenly a series of increasingly violent tremors pass through his body. Is he having a fit, is he dying? I jump to my feet. But now, breathing regularly, his face serene, his eyes shut, he lies seemingly asleep.

Are you really glad?

Really glad? What do you mean?'

That Beryl and I are now such good friends?

Of course I am. I hated it when you used to shout at her and insult her.

I often call her my best friend. To myself, to her. Does that surprise you?

No.

Does that make you jealous?

Of course not.

Are you sure? Of all of you, you were always the closest of my children.

Of course I'm sure.

His sufferings are becoming unbearable to me.

As soon as I have taken off my coat and sat down, he says: 'There's something I want to say to you at once.'

'Yes?'

'I want you to do something for me.'

'Anything. What is it?'

'I want you to speak to the specialist – what's-his-name – the one with the house in the Algarve.' His memory has begun to flake away in disconnected shards.

'What about?'

'I want you to ask him to give me an injection.'

'An injection?' I suddenly feel chilled.

'To finish me off.'

'I can't do that.' I shake my head from side to side repeatedly.

'*Please!*'

'No, no! He'd be horrified at the suggestion. And in any case – how could I, your daughter…?'

'Doctors do those things. You know they do those things.'

'Sorry. No. No, certainly not.'

He gives a dry, gasping laugh. The effort of it contorts his face, his teeth suddenly seem far too large for his mouth. 'Ring up the vet then!'

He must be joking, I tell myself. But I cannot be sure.

Later, as I gaze across at his motionless body, the silent interrogation resumes.

I have another idea. Couldn't you do it?

Me?

This is hell and I am in it? Quotation. Where's it from?

Faustus.

Oh, clever girl! You were always the cleverest of the brood. Don't you want to release me from my hell?

Oh, father… I hate to see you suffer. But there's this taboo. It's too strong.

Taboo? What taboo?

It's as though you were asking me to have sex with you. I – I just can't help you – much though I want to. Oh, please understand.

It would be so easy. Wouldn't it?

That's what makes it so difficult.

I am thinking die, die, die, willing it but incapable of bringing it about, when Beryl enters the room. She looks at me, she looks at him. Then she crosses over and takes his wrist in her hand. She takes away the hand and places it on his forehead. She is staring at me.

'It's horrible to see him suffer like this.'

'The trouble is that he's so strong,' she says. 'That's the trouble. I was reading in the paper the other day of a man who was in the Foreign Legion and then took to crime. The police cornered him and he shot at them. So they shot back. It took six bullets before they'd killed him. He's like that, your poor dad.' She looks down at it him. Appraising him, a miracle – or freak – of nature.

There is a long silence, as we stare at each other. She pulls out one of the pillows from under him, pats it vigorously and then replaces it. She pulls out the other pillow, but, instead of patting it and replacing it, she holds it against her ample breasts with both her hands. It might be a child to which she is giving suck.

Then the silent interrogation begins, no longer between him and me but between her and me.

Have you reached the end of your tether?

Yes, yes, yes! I can't take any more. And he reached the end of his tether long, long ago.

Do you want me to do it for you?

Please. Oh, yes, please.

Truly?

Yes, truly.

Now?

Now. At once. Please, please.

Time had stopped. Now it resumes. She moves towards him with the pillow. Her face is calm, tender, determined. She lowers the pillow. I turn away my head.

At the graveside she is on the other side of the grave. I hardly hear the priest's valedictory words. I stare across at her. Most of the family are in dark clothes. My own coat is black. But she is wearing a tent-like sky-blue coat wrapped round her generous body and a white hat with a sky-blue feather in it. Her high cheekbones are glistening as the sunlight shines on them. Is she sweating or is she crying?

I slip around the grave, away from Roy and the children, and stand beside her. Yes, she is crying. I put out my hand. She takes it. She imprisons it.

Death by Water

Luke had never been interested in art – in photography, yes, with all the ardour of a besotted amateur, but never, never art. What changed that was Lydia's postcard.

His first thought was how odd it was that, rather than writing a letter, she should have scribbled her condolence almost diagonally on a picture postcard. But then she had always been odd and had become increasingly so since their divorce, amicable though that had been. With no preamble, the message at once began: 'I can't stop thinking about you in your tragic and truly ghastly loss. Don't hesitate to call on me, please, *please*. I never had any bitterness towards Joy, none whatever, please believe that. Such a lovely person. Fondest thoughts. L.' Underneath she had scribbled: 'Carrie joins me in this.' Carrie was their daughter, of whom Lydia had custody.

When he had turned the postcard over, Luke thought Lydia's behaviour even odder. It showed a drowned woman, floating on a stream with her hands raised as though to welcome or even, yes, supplicate imminent death. The picture was a famous one but he did not recognise it. He peered. It was in the Tate Gallery, he read. It was entitled *Ophelia*. The painter, whose name was vaguely familiar but of whom he knew nothing at all, was given as J.E. Millais.

That she should have chosen that picture, whether consciously or unconsciously, made Lydia's perfunctory condolence not merely odder but also, all at once, disturbing. What was she at? *Don't hesitate to call on me.* That was something that, after such a postcard, he would never, ever do.

47

And yet ... Did she perhaps imagine that that serene, resigned image of the pale face and even paler arms surrounded by all those summer flowers and by the outspread clothes that kept the lifeless body afloat, would bring him some kind of consolation?

He chucked the card into the waste-paper basket. He had kept all the other expressions of condolence but that card he would not keep. Then he stooped, retrieved it, and with panicky, violent gestures, tore it into scraps. As soon as he had done so, he wished that he could undo the action. He wanted to look again at the woman with the pale, uplifted arms and the pale, serene face.

He climbed the narrow, precipitous steps up to the attic that he now always called 'the photograph room'. It was a Saturday and he had decided to devote the whole of the weekend to work that he planned to submit for an exhibition of photographs of the borough in which he lived. But he could not concentrate, he kept making mistakes. He thought, with both bewilderment and rising indignation, of Lydia's choice of *that* picture to express her condolences on the death of the woman who had usurped her. Then, repeatedly, however hard he attempted to halt them, images began to flash on and off on the retina of his memory, like photographs projected in rapid succession on to a screen. Seen from every angle, they were of that body once so familiar to him and then, when he had had to identify it in the morgue, all at once grown strange and threatening.

The morgue was little more than a squat concrete shed, stinking of formaldehyde and lined on one side with what looked like outsize, rusty refrigerators and on the other, mysteriously, with a row of upright chairs set out as though for spectators yet to arrive. Joy had been horrendously battered and bruised by the waves that had hurled her against the rocks. Her body was swollen and livid with a rainbow of colours – green, yellow, red, purple. Having made the identification, he had rushed outside into the searing sunlight, there to vomit beside a gaunt, straggly bush, a hand clutching its stem while two barefoot urchins in ragged clothes, a boy and a girl, watched him with dispassionate curiosity. The violence of his retching brought tears to his eyes.

In a corner of the attic there was a dilapidated chaise-longue. It had belonged to Joy's mother. Although it was in such bad condition, Joy had insisted that they keep it after her mother's death – 'It has memories', she had said. What those memories were she had never specified and he had never asked. He had always felt vaguely uncomfortable with Joy's mother. He now felt uncomfortable even with her memory. He went over to the chaise-longue, sank down on it, and covered his eyes with his hands. But the images persisted.

'Excuse me – is that your lady? Yes?' The Moroccan official with the dull, sleepy eyes, the lethargic gait and slurred intonation that had made Luke briefly wonder if he were drunk, had put a hand on his shoulder. 'Yes?' the man had repeated.

Luke had wanted to say: 'No, it's not my lady.' How could that swollen, lacerated mass of multi-coloured flesh be the woman to whom he had made love only the night before? But he had eventually nodded. 'Yes,' he had whispered. Then, having cleared his throat, more loudly: 'Yes.'

Now he saw the image that, of all the many images, had shocked him the most. It was a close-up. In black and white. Teeth smashed, nose flattened. She had had such beautiful teeth, large, regular. They had given her ready smile its extraordinary radiance. Resting his head against the tattered, dusty grey velvet of the chaise-longue, he pressed his fingers against his eyeballs as though to squeeze out the ghastly, ghostly image lodged behind them.

He heard the official ask: 'Excuse me, sir. Your wife – did she go out alone?'

'Yes, yes. There was something wrong with my camera – one of my cameras. I was trying to repair it. She said that she wanted to go for a walk.'

'Perhaps she climbed up some rocks and fell into the sea.'

'Perhaps. It would have been dark.'

'It was foolish to go for a walk in the dark. A lady. Alone. That is not a good place in the dark.'

The questioning had continued, with other officials, some more sympathetic, some less so and some blatantly hostile, asking their questions. Why, why, why? He did not know why. They had not even had a quarrel before she went out. She had kissed him on the cheek and then on the forehead, bending over him. He had had the camera in his hands. The kissing had distracted him – and, yes, faintly irritated him. He must get the winding mechanism of that old Leica to work properly. Otherwise his holiday would be ruined. It was his favourite camera. If he could not fix it, then it was unlikely that he would find anyone in this little town who could do so.

With a tardiness that now, back in England, amazed him, it had taken him a long time to realise that all these seemingly random questions were directed to one monstrous end. Had he himself killed her? When they finally gave up, he knew that they had done so not because he had convinced them that he was innocent but because they could not prove that he was guilty.

Again, fingertips pressed against his eyes, he tried to stop the flicker of horrific image on image. *Think of something else.* All at once he thought of Lydia's postcard. He had looked at it for only a few seconds before tearing it into fragments, but miraculously he could remember every detail. That was how death should be: serene, resigned, even welcoming, with the waters showing no violence to the body consigned to them but only a tender acceptance. Yes, that was how it should be. Easeful death should be easeful. He opened his eyes and stared up through the skylight at the clear, pale-blue sky. For the first time since his visit to the morgue, he felt miraculously assuaged. He thought of his convulsive vomiting outside the morgue. It was as though a similar bout of vomiting had now at last relieved his body of all the poisons that had caused him so much agony and malaise over the past five weeks.

He sought out Millais on the internet, and was amazed that there should be so much about someone of whom he – an educated man, he liked to think – knew absolutely nothing. He even summoned up the image of the picture on his screen. Repeatedly he ran forefinger and middle finger over it, caressing now the pale face, now the pale hands, and now the body encased, as though after an embalment, in all that rich fabric. The screen felt hard to the touch. It felt cold when, in a moment of crazy abandon, he put his lips to the face at its centre.

He went to the Tate, not visited since the days when he and Lydia, both students, would go there on a Saturday or Sunday afternoon if, for one reason or another, they could not play the tennis that at that time was their chief recreation. The long, high-ceilinged room was empty except for the black male attendant at the far end of it and an elderly American woman, with coarse grey hair and a pronounced stoop, talking to him in a loud voice not about the pictures but about her problems with London Transport. Motionless, he stared fixedly at the white oval of the face, with the eyes open in what might have been a trance, not death. Again, as on that day when Lydia's postcard had arrived, the image had an extraordinarily consoling and assuaging effect on him. He would like to have touched it, as he had touched and then kissed the face on the computer screen. 'Yes,' he whispered. Then more loudly: 'Yes, yes!'

The attendant and the woman halted in their conversation and, heads turned, peered down the long gallery at him. Then the woman shrugged, pulled a little face at the attendant and resumed what she had been saying.

From a book purchased on the internet from a second-hand dealer in Boston, he learned that Millais had painted the background of the picture by the Hogsmill River, near a place called Ewell. What had then been a remote village had now become a grindingly busy suburb of London. In search of the right setting for what many believed to be his masterpiece, Millais had taken up residence in the village with another painter, Holman Hunt, who, like Millais himself, had never been more than a name to Luke. Many years later Hunt had recorded how Millais for a whole day had 'walked along beaten lanes and jumped over ditches and ruts without finding a place that would satisfy him'. Then he had come on exactly what he wanted: overarching trees, scarcely stirring waters, a richness of grass, reeds and flowers. He had cried out to his companion: 'Look! Could anything be more perfect?' Hunt remarked, as many were to do, on Millais's luck in coming on the place on his first day of searching. Throughout his life Millais was generally acknowledged to be a spoiled favourite of luck.

Having learned all this, Luke was overcome by an obsessive longing to find the place. He planned to go on the very next Saturday, but then was obliged, because of the illness of a colleague, to agree at the last moment to show a Hampstead house, several months now on the market, to a prospective buyer from France. He was conscientious about his work. He knew that a partnership in the long established firm of estate agents was almost in his grasp. He must not jeopardise that.

He thought of the Sunday but Carrie was due to spend it with him, as she did once every four weeks. Couldn't he put her off? No. He was conscientious not merely about his work but also about his erratic and often clumsy relationship with this nine-year-old girl who could never forgive him for, as she saw it, abandoning not merely her mother but also herself. So it had to be the following Saturday.

Of course he took his two favourite cameras, the ancient Leica and the new digital Canon, a scientific miracle. In his biography, Millais's son had quoted from a letter written by his father to a woman friend. In it, the painter described how, day after day, he had sat in extreme discomfort under an umbrella, 'being blown by the wind into the water', and so gradually becoming 'intimate with the feelings of Ophelia when that lady sank to muddy death.' But as Luke stepped off the train at Ewell – a totally unremarkable place, he thought – there was not a breath of wind and the sun was hot and dazzling. He felt a surge of excitement flood through his body, making his cheeks flush and his finger-tips tingle. He might have been on his way to some long awaited, desperately wanted assignation.

He knew by now that a young and beautiful woman had lain for hours on end in an enamel bath tub filled with water inadequately warmed by a lamp placed beneath it, to model for Ophelia. She had caught pleurisy and it was thought that that might well have precipitated the pulmonary tuberculosis from which she had suffered for the rest of her cruelly short life. Nonetheless, Luke all but expected to come not merely on the reach of water that had provided Millais with his setting but also on Ophelia herself, her eyes wide open, her lips slightly parted, and one of those white, raised hands grasping a water-lily.

He repeatedly paused as he followed the winding course of what often became little more than a stream. Could this be the place? This? This? Each time he decided : No. One curve seemed exactly right. But in the distance some youths, most them stripped to their waists, were playing football, shouting to each other in a language that Luke could not understand or even identify. Their strident voices and the thud, thud, thud of the ball robbed the location of any intimacy or peace. It was the same at a stretch where the foliage was particularly green and luxuriant and the trees arched over the water exactly as in the picture. But on the opposite bank two people, a girl and a boy, were lying out on the lush grass with a transistor radio blaring out. A male voice seemed to be bawling 'Wow, wow, wow!' endlessly over and over again. Luke hated that sort of music. As students and later in the first years of their marriage, he and Lydia had stood stoically evening after evening at Promenade concerts throughout a whole scorching summer. At each 'Wow!' something huge and cumbersome jarred within him, making him feel vaguely giddy and nauseous.

Then at long last, sweat darkening his pale blue shirt under the armpits and glistening on his forehead, he suddenly reached a place, shadowed by overarching trees and the grass almost waist-high, that made him at once say to himself, with a mingling of relief and triumph, 'Yes, yes, this is it!' He had searched in vain in books and on the internet for the exact location at which Millais had sat on his stool before his easel. But he had absolutely no doubt that this was where it was.

Here the often narrow river was unusually wide as it curved in its negotiation of a dumpy hillock surmounted by three elder trees. The contrast between the emaciated near-nudity of those trees and the green luxuriance of the willows on the opposite bank was startling. Perhaps it was on that hillock that Millais had set up stool, easel and umbrella as the rain fell relentlessly and he no less relentlessly worked at his masterpiece. In the otherwise symmetrical curve there was another, far smaller curve, where a tributary stream – yes, the brook, the brook, he thought, of Gertrude's valedictory description – joined the river. Millais must have at once decided that that location was exactly right. That was what people had meant when they talked of his luck.

Hands on hips Luke stared from the coign of the hillock, with its dry, yellow grass and skeletal trees, across at the luxuriant arbour opposite. Then he glanced to right and left, on the other side of the bank. Far off to the right a tall, middle-aged man in a dark suit – how hot he must feel and how ridiculous to dress like that on a day like this! – was meandering along the tow path, a camera slung round his neck. A fellow photographer, perhaps even a rival. Nearer, to the left, a woman sprawled out in a deck-chair, a red bug of a car parked behind her in the shade. Two small girls, dressed only in what at this distance looked liked white knickers, were playing in the shallows. From time to time the wind carried their excited voices and laughter over to him. But the sounds did not disturb him in the least, as first the sounds of the thudding football and the foreign male voices and then of the blaring transistor radio had done.

He lowered his rucksack and took out the Leica. Bought second hand, it dated from a period when he had still not been born. By contemporary standards it was primitive. But it was the camera that he treasured the most. The difference between using it and the Canon was the difference between driving an ancient Rolls Royce with a manual gearshift and a new Honda with automatic transmission, he had often thought. In the first case, troublesome though it was, one had so much more control over precisely what one was doing.

But on this occasion he felt dissatisfied with the Leica. As he first calculated distance and then, holding out the meter, aperture and shutter speed, he realised that that leafy, flowery bower of the painting was too far away. He needed the Canon and its powerful telephoto lens. He sighed, replaced the one camera, took up the other. Then, as he gazed at the screen of the Canon, he all at once had the demented illusion that something at once devastating and exhilarating had happened. There, in the centre, a figure lay out for him on the quiet water, hands and face pale, eyes open as if in a trance, robes heavy around her and yet never dragging her down into the chilly depths and so out of sight. But the figure was not that of the beautiful, doomed woman who had lain for hours on end in lukewarm water in a bathtub. Instead, it was that of another beautiful, doomed woman, his wife, his Joy. He gasped. Then frenetically he began clicking. As he did so the figure slowly bled out of the image on the screen, until the arbour was once again no more than a stretch of water overhung by willows and surrounded by reeds and flowers. That he had suffered such an obvious hallucination alarmed him. It showed the depth and distraction of his grief.

He continued to take photographs now from this angle and now from that. At one point, kneeling on the grass, he had to replace the by now exhausted film with another. He laboured to the top of the knoll and took a photograph from that vantage. Then he slithered down it. He changed cameras and again took some photographs with the Leica. He knew that those would be inferior, but he persisted out of loyalty to his ancient favourite.

He hardly heard the car that was lurching and swerving over hummocks of grass as it approached. But he turned as its engine abruptly cut out, and first one door slammed and then the other.

'Excuse me, sir.'

'Yes?'

Two uniformed police officers, a tall, gaunt man and a tiny, tubby woman with large calves, were walking towards him. It was the tall, gaunt man who had spoken. Even though the pace of the couple was so leisurely, Luke had a sense of stealthy menace. Suddenly he felt afraid, as he had suddenly felt afraid when in Morocco the official had asked him why he had not accompanied Joy on her last, fatal walk along the beach at night.

'May I ask what you are doing, sir?

'Well, taking photographs. As you can see.' He held up the Canon.

'May I have that, sir?' The policeman   extended a large hand. Luke noticed that the band of the wedding-ring on its fourth finger was unusually broad. Luke surrendered the camera. Later, he was to wonder why he had done so with such submissiveness.

'What's all this about?' he asked as the man handed the camera to the diminutive woman. She would have been pretty if it had not been for the almost total absence of any eyebrows.

It was the woman who answered the question. 'We had a complaint,' she said. 'By mobile.' She had an oddly metallic voice and her diction was so precise that it sounded almost prim. Each word was like a small stone being dropped, at regular intervals, into a tin.

'A complaint? What am I supposed to have been doing?'

The man now replied. 'Over there.' He pointed across the river. 'Those two kids. Someone complained that you were spending a long, long time photographing them.'

'What absolute nonsense! I wasn't photographing them. I was hardly aware of them.'

'Then what were you doing?'

'I was photographing that bend of the river. That's all.'

'And why should you be doing that?' Again it was the small stones falling into the tin.

'Because that's where a famous artist painted his most famous picture.'

'And who would that be?' the man asked in a voice of disbelieving sarcasm.

'He was called Millais – J.E. Millais. The painting was called '*Ophelia*'. It was here that he sat. On a stool. At his easel. It rained all the time. He used to have an umbrella open above him.'

The man might not have been listening. Again he held out his hand: 'May I have the other camera, sir?'

Luke hesitated. The man stooped and jerked it out of the rucksack. Then he said: 'I'm afraid you'll have to come with us.'

'Come with you?' Luke was incredulous.

'Yes, sir. To help us with our enquiries. If we have a complaint of this seriousness, then we have to investigate it. Fully.'

'But what have I done?'

There was no answer.

'Better come along, sir,' the woman said. 'No point in wasting time.'

The small house was crowded with people. Luke might have had more acceptances than expected to a party.

A policewoman, not the one encountered by the river, peered at a photograph in a silver frame on the mantelpiece. She picked it up and peered at it even more closely. 'And who might this be?' she asked in a heavy Scottish accent.

'My daughter?'

'Your *daughter*?'

'Yes, my daughter.'

'Why has she got nothing on?'

'There was a heat wave. We — she, her mother, I — were in the back garden. That garden's not in the least overlooked. You can see for yourself.' He wished that he did not sounds so flustered.

'How old was she at the time?'

'Five.'

'Where is she now?' a male officer behind her put in.

'With her mother. We're divorced now. She has custody.'

'*She* has custody?'

Luke nodded.

'Why should that be?'

'Well, that was what the court decided. And my second wife and I didn't oppose the decision. That seemed the best for Carrie — for my daughter.'

'And where is your second wife?' the woman demanded.

'Dead.'

'Dead?'

'Yes. Dead. She died seven weeks ago.' His voice was now also dead.

Remorselessly they went through drawer after drawer in their ravenous appetite for anything put down on paper. 'I'm afraid we'll have to take this,' one or other of them would say, holding up a file or a packet of letters. They also announced that they would have to remove his two computers, all his disks, and the photographs so carefully stored in boxes in the garage.

'But I need that,' he repeatedly protested. Or: 'But that has nothing to do with my private life. That's only to do with my work.'

Sometimes one of them vouchsafed an expressionless: 'Sorry'. Sometimes there was no response at all.

Eventually, in a state of despair, incredulity and rage, he collapsed on to a sofa and let them get on with their task.

After they had bagged or boxed everything and were about to leave him, he asked: 'And how long are you going to keep all these things?'

'For as long as is necessary,' the officer in charge replied.

'And how long is that?'

The officer shrugged. 'As long as it takes.'

One of the women volunteered: 'Your guess is as good as ours.'

At the door Luke said: 'Why did that woman complain to you? What got into her? This sort of thing has become a crazy obsession with people. I'm not interested in children, never have been, never, never. For God's sake I've been married – married twice.'

'We can't reveal our sources' the officer in charge replied. 'If there's a complaint, we have to act on it.'

They went on with their stacking of the bags and boxes in their van. Then an officer appeared carrying the desktop, immediately followed by another carrying the laptop. 'Don't worry. No harm will come to these,' the second said. 'We have our experts.'

'But I can't do without them. I need them.'

He had said it before. This time he might not have spoken. No one paid any attention, as they continued to hurry about their tasks.

Once again Luke had slept only fitfully. At one point, soon after four, he had even got up and decided to play some music. But the CD of the music that he most wanted to hear, the slow of movement of the Elgar piano quintet – so sublimely reposeful and consolatory, he had always thought – was mysteriously not in its place in the rack by his bed. Feverishly he had once again searched, eventually causing a number of disks to cascade to the floor. Oh fuck, fuck, fuck! He had stooped to retrieve them. The Schumann Violin Concerto wasn't there, either. Those bloody idiots must have taken the disks by mistake. It was crazy, it was idiotic. He couldn't even listen to the music that he wanted to. And if he now wished to send an e-mail, he had to trek out to the cyber café in the High Street. People had talked of Millais's luck. How about his own ill-luck?

Later Carrie, who was on one of her weekend visits, and he sat out on the lawn of the little back-garden, having breakfast. Luke stared up at the sky as he munched on a slice of toast that he had managed to burn. It was so crisp that fragments scattered down from his mouth on to his shirt.

'What's the matter, daddy?

'The matter? Nothing. I couldn't sleep. That's all.' He had told no one of his trouble with the police. Irrationally, although he was totally innocent, he felt both guilt and shame.

'*Something's* the matter.' Lydia was often remarking, with a mixture of pride and anxiety, that Carrie was so grown-up for her age. She was right. Now the girl leaned across the table: 'Daddy, what is it? Tell me.'

He pondered, again biting on to what had once been a slice of bread but was now a charred rusk. Again fragments scattered downwards. His mouth filled with a bitter dryness. He felt that he was choking. He put a hand to his forehead. 'I suppose I'm sad,' he said. 'How can I not be sad? Nothing seems right. It's all gone. Everything. I'm sad.' His lower lip briefly trembled.

'Oh, daddy!' Impulsively she put a hand over his. He looked down, realising that she was once again biting her nails, as she had started to do when he and her mother had first agreed on a divorce. She jumped to her feet. He thought that she was going to come round the table to comfort to him. He would have welcomed that. It might have bridged the gulf that now seemed always to gape between them.

But, distracted, she suddenly swerved away. 'Good morning, Mr Thai!' All her attention was now focused not on him but on the Siamese cat. Tail erect and blank, pale-blue eyes blinking at the sunlight, he had come out through the kitchen door. He let out a miaow and then another, louder one.

'Oh, Mr Thai, you're always hungry! What's the matter with you. Have you got worms? Wait a moment, darling. I'll get you something.'

She walked into the kitchen and the cat padded after her. Luke put his head in his hands.

'I'm glad to be able to tell you that our investigations have now been concluded and that we have decided not to proceed any further.' The middle-aged, moustached officer in his too short grey trousers and dark-blue blazer with brass buttons might have been a Navy officer who had taken early retirement. Behind him stood a wispy young man in a brown suit, who stared at Luke with a disconcerting fixedness.

'Well, that's really big of you. How kind! And can you tell me when I can have back my computers – and my files – and my photographs – and my letters. That might make life a little more convenient for me. That might make it a little easier for me to get on with my job.'

'I can get a van to drop them off tomorrow afternoon, sir. That's what I was just going to propose. If you're likely to be in and if that's convenient for you.'

'I can certainly arrange to be in.'

'Then that's agreed. Tomorrow. Some time between two and five-thirty.'

'This person – this person who made these ludicrous accusation … I'd be very grateful if you could now let me have –'

'I'm afraid that's out of the question, sir. It's not our policy in cases of this kind to reveal the identity of an informant. For obvious reasons.'

'Don't you think I'm owed an apology?'

The man shrugged. 'Just as we cannot reveal an informant's name and address, so we never reveal the name and address of the, er, accused party until a charge has been laid. So it would be impossible for any informant to get in touch even if he – or she – wished to do so. In this case, no charge has been laid. Or will be laid.'

'Then how about an apology from you lot?'

'From us, sir?'

'Yes. From the police. A formal apology. After all, you've put me through a hell of a lot of anxiety and inconvenience.'

'I don't think you fully understand, sir. If I may say so. If we receive a complaint of this kind, then it is only our duty to investigate. Thoroughly, impartially. That is what we did. We have now decided that you have no case to answer. That's the end of the matter.'

'So no one apologises for a total cock-up? Is that what you're telling me?'

The man gave a twitchy smile and a little bow, as though in affirmation. Then he said: 'The van will be with you tomorrow afternoon.' He turned away. 'Goodbye, sir,' he said over his shoulder. 'And thank you.'

As Luke walked down the steps of the Town Hall into the downpour, someone said his name. He turned. It was a tall, middle-aged man with an umbrella raised in a hand, while the other hand rested on the camera that dangled from his neck.

'I wanted to congratulate you. You deserved more than a commendation. You ought to have won.'

Luke laughed. He agreed with the man but felt no bitterness. 'Nothing in life is fair.'

'How right you are! Few of us get our deserts.' The man was now close beside him. He smelled of something cloying and sweetish. Luke himself never used any sort deodorant or aftershave. 'I'm a photographer myself. In an amateur way.'

'That's all I am. An amateur.'

'But an amateur with a professional touch.'

They were now walking down the street, with the man holding the umbrella more over Luke than over himself.

'Why didn't you submit something yourself?'

'Oh, I take my photographs only for my own pleasure. A private hobby.' The voice had not so much a stammer as an intermittent hesitation.

'How did you come to know my name? Have we met before?'

'I overheard someone introducing you to someone else. You were sitting just in front of me during the prize announcements. I'd noticed you already.' He paused. 'Your face was – familiar.'

'What an idiot I was not to bring an umbrella or raincoat! If you don't take a bigger share of your umbrella, you're going to get horribly wet.'

'Why don't we have a drink at my place until it's all over? It's just round the corner from here. Left at the pillar box.'

Luke hesitated. 'Well … All right. That's kind of you.'

The steep steps of the Edwardian block of flats were slithery from the rain. The entrance hall was large and dimly lit. Two upright, bentwood chairs flanked a cumbersome oak table. Othewise the whole area was bare.

'The lift's not working. D'you mind walking up?'

'Fine.'

The hand on the banister ahead of Luke was white and bony, the fingers unusually long with nails curving over them, in urgent need of cutting. At random, the umbrella dripped water now on to one step and now on to another. The man began to wheeze as they started on the flight up to the third floor. He must be asthmatic, Luke decided. 'Nothing bloody works in this block. And do the landlords care? Of course not. But I'm a statutory tenant and so I can't complain. I pay about a third of what almost everyone else does.'

They stopped outside the front door and the man fumbled in a pocket of his unusually long and voluminous black raincoat and pulled out his keys. The door open, he turned to allow Luke to enter ahead of him. He gave a little bow. 'Welcome to my humble abode.'

The sitting-room, frowsty, as dimly lit as the downstairs hall and crowded with pieces of Victorian and Edwardian furniture too large for it, reminded Luke of visits to his mother's widowed mother, during his childhood. Then two totally incongruous objects caught his eye. One was a pinball machine, standing in one corner. The other was a juke-box. standing in another. Oddly, both were garishly lit up.

The man smiled and, throwing out an arm, said: 'This – with one or two exceptions – is all my dear, deceased mother's taste. I was too lazy – and too broke – to do anything about it after she had gone.' Hs surveyed the room, turning his head from side to side, as though in a first appraisal. Then he urged: 'Now sit down – there – or there – or anywhere you like – and let me fix you a drink. What would you fancy?'

Luke had noticed a bottle labelled Oloroso Sherry on a sideboard. 'Some sherry?'

'Why not? I think sherry wine would be just the thing on a miserable night like this.'

The man poured out a glass of sherry and handed it to Luke. 'I hope that's not too sweet for you. That's my vulgar taste, I'm afraid, not my mother's.'

Luke sipped. 'Fine.'

The man put down his glass and walked across to a desk. He pulled open a drawer and took out a photograph.

'That may amuse you.' He crossed over to Luke and held it out.

With reluctant foreboding, Luke slowly took it and looked down. Executed with a professionalism similar to the one on which he prided himself, it showed a tall, broad-shouldered man with close-cropped hair holding an ancient Leica up to his face. Behind him were three elder trees. In front of him there was the wide curve of a river, glittering in the sunlight. The unseen photographer had clearly used a powerful telescopic lens.

'Good, don't you think? It was difficult to be sure of getting that contrast between the bareness of the trees and all that foliage on the bank. I'm pleased with it.'

'You were the person who ...' Luke spoke in wonder.'I remember ... a man in a dark suit.'

'Yes, I'd come on from a funeral. My mother's in fact. I was dreadfully hot. Wasn't that a beautiful day?' The man lowered himself into the vast, over-upholstered, chintz-covered armchair that faced the identical one in which Luke was still gazing down at the photograph with a mixture of amazement and dread. 'You know, I recognised you at once when I saw you at the Town Hall. I lied to you just now. I'd entered three photographs. But − no luck. When I recognised you I at once took that chair behind you. Then I heard that man greet you. An extraordinary coincidence, I thought. But it's not really all that extraordinary, is it? We have things in common. We're both amateur photographers for one. We're both about the same age. We look so much like each other that we might almost pass for brothers. And then' − he smiled, revealing small, irregular teeth − 'we have our other interest. I don't mean photography. I mean that more, er, esoteric one. Our hobby'

Luke stared at him, as though trying to remember where, many, many years ago, he had met this character.

' I feel terrible about it now,' the man said. 'I don't know what came over me. There is something that one both cherishes and hates in oneself. One wants to safeguard it and yet kill it. You know what I mean? You must do. You must know the experience.'

'I have no idea what you mean.'

'Of course you do. Why can't we be frank with each other?' The man tilted his head on one side. He looked at Luke with what was all too clearly understanding and affection. 'As I say − I can't think what got into me. What I did to you was, I suppose, what I really wanted to do to myself. Revelation, punishment. It was crazy, of course. Unforgiveable. I must have put you through hell. It was really quite a relief to me when I learned that the fuzz had decided to take things no further.' He laughed. 'It must have been one hell of a relief to you too.'

'You bastard! God − you bastard!'

'Yes. You're right. Absolutely right. One hundred percent. I apologise. I grovel. It was odd − as soon as I saw you − photographing,

photographing, in that same spot – with those two little ones ... I knew, I just *knew*!'

Luke lunged forward and grabbed the man by the lapels of his jacket. In a frenzy he dragged him to his feet and then punched him repeatedly – on the chin, on the mouth, cutting his knuckles on those small, irregular teeth, on the nose, causing a snake of blood to wriggle slowly out of a nostril. Then something stopped him. It was the maniacal glee glittering from the man's previously dull, sad eyes, and the way that he kept whispering, 'Yes, yes, *yes,*' in an endless crescendo.

Luke pushed the man so that he toppled back into the arm-chair. Then the man was laughing as the words jerked out of him: 'You don't mean to say ...? Did I get it all wrong? ... Is that what you're trying – rather too brutally – to tell me?'

Luke kicked out, the toe-cap of this shoe catching the other's knee-cap. There was a dry sound at the impact, like a rifle shot heard from far away. Then he rushed to the front door, pulled it open and strode out. Having descended three steps at what was almost a run, he returned and pulled the door shut.

He raced down the staircase into the darkness and rain. Head lowered, he ran down the almost totally deserted street. By the municipal library, only two of its windows, high up in the façade, still lit, he took is usual short-cut across its triangular courtyard. Usually, even as late as this, there would be skate-boarders rattling and thudding over its paving. But now there was no one. A street-lamp illuminated miniature lakes of water, between which he zigzagged. Then, all at once, he slackened his pace, approached one of the benches in front of the building, and sank down on to it, gasping for breath. God, what a shit! What a shit! He ought to have killed him. Suddenly he thought of the cleaner ('quickly digests organic matter such as hair, paper, grease, rice, pasta, soap, fabric, fat, slime etc.) bought at the request of his charming, fat, inefficient Colombian char, mother of five children, for the bathrom basin only the day before. *Quickly digests slime ... CAUTION. Contains sulphuric acid.* That would do the trick.

Then, abruptly, that fantasy died. All at once tiredness overwhelmed him. Despite the savage downpour, he stretched himself out on the bench and stared for several seconds up at the livid, lowering sky. He closed his eyes. He felt the water trickling through his hair and sidling under his collar on to the flesh beneath it. He tasted it, cool and faintly metallic, on his lips. It was in his nostrils, even in his ears. It was wonderfully cleansing, wonderfully soothing, wonderfully consoling.

He had the illusion that he was now lying not on a hard bench, its struts digging into his shoulder blades and haunches, but on a quiet stream, drifting on and on under a velvety, star-studded sky to total oblivion.

Then a dog barked. Barked again. He jerked up, swung down his feet. An old, bowed, hooded man, with a dripping black-and-white mongrel on a long lead, was passing. 'Shurrup! Shurrup!' the man shouted at the dog. Then: 'Sorry about that,' he said in a hoarse voice to Luke. 'He's a real idiot. Always barking, barking, barking at nothing.'

Luke got to his feet and began to trudge on through the darkness and downpour.

The Appeal

She stepped over one puddle. She stepped over a larger one. She winced on the second occasion, as though she had twisted her ankle. But in fact she had merely landed on one side of her shoe. The new laptop that they had just given her seemed heavier than the old one. They had said that she would find it much more convenient, but it was certainly not more convenient now. She had thought at the time that they had given it to her as a reward for always refusing, unlike some of the other adjudicators, to be bamboozled by a succession of shifty, shameless appellants. But at this moment it felt more like a punishment.

She had just spoken to Jake on her mobile.

'Oh, Maddy, wait a mo. I've got gunge all over my fingers. Let me wipe them. Sorry! I've been throwing a pot.'

'I'd like to throw a pot at you, you bastard!' She laughed, to indicate that she was joking. But she was not joking, and he knew that.

'Oh, Maddy, don't get mad at me!' Had she really once thought his feeble word-play funny? Had she really once thought his American accent attractive? 'What's the matter? What have I done?'

'The car. Didn't you notice the petrol gauge?' In her hurry that morning she had also failed to notice it.

'What's the matter with it?'

'What's usually the matter with a petrol gauge?

'Oh, you don't mean…?"

67

'I'm stranded. And I've got to be in that bloody court in another ten minutes.'

'Oh, Maddy!'

'I want you to get to that car a.s.p. Have it filled up. Then leave it outside the court by three o'clock at the latest. I'm taking a bus – *now* – if there is a bus. But I don't intend to take a bus to pick up the kids. So get the car to the court. Got it?'

'Yeah. Sorry, Maddy. Don't get mad at me.'

The repetition of the pun maddened her even more. 'Now listen carefully. This is where I left it.' She told him, and then repeated the instructions. 'And remember to take the keys.'

'Of course I'll take them. Oh, Maddy...'

Decisively, she cut him off.

Maddy stepped over another puddle. She saw the bus stop and, standing at the far back of the shelter, a bowed old woman in scuffed, low-heeled brogues, a plastic macintosh and a beret. Her face was as grey and shiny as the macintosh and her watery eyes were of the same washed-out blue as the beret's. The woman jerked her head up as Maddy approached, frowned and then gave a lop-sided, anxious smile.

'Excuse me. Do you know anything about these buses?' She had her right arm in a sling and the right side of her face was frozen. A stroke, Maddy thought. That would explain the smile

'Very little.'

'What I want to know is whether the 119 passes Budgen's. I think my brother told me the 119 was the one I had to take. But I may have got it wrong. Perhaps he said the 111. Both seem to stop here.'

Maddy shifted her weight from one long, lithe leg to the other and the laptop from under her left arm to under her right. 'Budgen's?'

'My brother told me to get out at Budgen's. It's a supermarket.'

Maddy knew that Budgen's was a supermarket, but she had never entered this particular Budgen's or any other Budgen's. 'If I've seen a Budgen's on this route, I don't remember it.'

'What I want is the – the – Appellate Court. Is that what it's called? I think so.'

'Well, the 119 is the bus for the Appellate Court.' Maddy did not add that she was going there herself.

The woman's whole body slumped in relief. 'Oh, that's good. I'm so worried that I may be late. Not that we know what time our case will be heard.'

Maddy perched herself on the red, backless plastic rail that now did uncomfortable service for the often-vandalised wooden bench that had once stood in its place. Her laptop rested on her lap. She took a handkerchief out of her coat pocket and raised it to the tip of her nose. She turned her head away from the woman. She did not want to prolong the conversation.

'My brother told me that he and his friend would fetch me. But it would have meant crossing the whole of London. My little house is in Kennington, you see, and they're in Highgate. So I told him I could easily find my own way. I'm used to the buses. I have my pass. I always say the only advantage of getting old is to have a travel pass. My latest is one of these Oyster things. At first I couldn't get used it but now I find it much more convenient. You don't even have to take it out of its wallet. With my disabilities, that's always difficult for me.'

Maddy said nothing. She wondered if the bus were going to be delayed much longer. She wondered if the old woman would go on and on with this inane chatter. She wondered if Jake would remember to take his keys when he went to deal with the car. It was lucky that today she had only the one case. The day before she had had an extra one in addition to the two already allotted to her, because one of the adjudicators had been ill. He was constantly falling ill. And he was a dead loss anyway. It was time, she often thought, that they gave him the push.

At last the bus arrived. Maddy stood aside for the old woman as, crab-like, she grasped the handle and, after two heaves, managed to struggle aboard with an 'Oops!' and then a deep sigh. Maddy had had a brief impulse to help her, then had decided not to do so. She now made a point of sitting as far away from her as possible. Why was the poor old thing going to the court? It must be as a witness.

When the bus arrived at the stop just beyond Budgen's, Maddy jumped off, without looking round to see what had happened to the old woman, and hurried away. People were going to talk enough nonsense for the rest of the day without having to put up with more of it now.

Maddy was efficient. She had scrupulously read every word of her two bundles for the day. She also remembered everything in them. *They* had told her what *they* expected her to do. Then the Home Office bundle had told her exactly how she was to do it. Her appellant's bundle had been far larger than the Home Office one. That was usually the case. Desperate asylum-seekers tended to jeopardise their appeals by going on and on and on, whereas employees of the Home Office, secure and confident in their lives, knew precisely when to stop.

When Maddy entered the office in which the adjudicators all gathered before going their separate ways to their courtrooms, she was glad to see that the colleague who had been absent yesterday had now returned. His complexion was muddy and his eyes dull. His jowls seemed to hang more loosely and fronds of his grey hair stuck to his scalp.

'Thank you for standing in for me.'

'Always happy to be of help.'

'I still feel absolutely ghastly.'

'You look absolutely ghastly.'

As, high heels clicking on the parquet, Maddy approached her court, she glimpsed the old woman outside it, sitting on a bench with an elderly, elongated man in a dark-blue pinstripe suit, the jacket sagging at the narrow shoulders and the trousers straining over a little paunch. There was a vague resemblance between the two – the same watery, washed-out blue eyes, the same bony hands, the same beaky noses. He must be the partner of the appellant, she decided, and she the sister whose name was on the order paper as the only other witness. The two of them could not enter the court to give their evidence until the appellant had been heard. The woman looked up at Maddy and gave that twitchy, lop-sided smile of hers. Maddy at once turned her head away.

Sometimes appellants imagined that it would help their cases if friends and relatives of theirs crowded the court. As far as Maddy was concerned, they were wrong about that, particularly if some of these supporters were children. Fortunately, today the court contained only herself, the appellant and the appellant's whiskery, grey-haired female barrister.

As Maddy entered, the barrister lurched to her feet and the appellant then did likewise. Maddy merely nodded as she took her place on the dais. She opened her laptop. As she listened to what, with patient assiduity, the gruff-voiced barrister was attempting to elicit from her seemingly reluctant client, Maddy also typed away, recording every sentence. But as her crimson-nailed fingers flicked at the keys, she was irritated that, after her previous laptop, this supposedly far superior replacement was putting up what she described later to Jake as 'a kind of passive resistance'. She prided herself on her speed and accuracy as a typist.

The appellant, a Moroccan, was a fleshy youth, his heavily oiled hair cut close to his skull. In his sulky, somnolent way, he was handsome. The Home Office had already decided that he was not a homosexual and she herself now at once also decided, with satisfaction, that they had been absolutely right. She had dealt with other such individuals – a Jamaican only last week, an Algerian a few weeks before – who claimed firstly that they were in long-term partnerships with British men and secondly that, as homosexuals, their lives would be in danger if they were deported back to their homelands.

Maddy knew, partly from experience and partly from what the Home Office bundle had told her, precisely what to ask the man. In no time at all, he became confused, contradicted himself repeatedly, and kept dawdling to silence while desperately searching for an answer. When at one moment she was needling him with particular finesse, he shouted, his voice suddenly hoarse and strangulated, 'Your question is racist!' The barrister jerked her head up and rolled her eyes, like a frightened horse. Maddy merely laughed and said: 'I don't think that's a helpful line for you to take.' But secretly she was furious. These days it was less offensive to be called a bitch than a racist.

The appellant's 'partner' – in her mind Maddy put the word in inverted commas – followed the Moroccan. He walked stiffly, one hand grasping a bony thigh as though he feared that it might snap under the pressure put on it by each footfall. Whenever he answered a question, he made a point of calling Maddy 'Madam'. On the first occasion she had thought, with momentary outrage, that he was using her first name. Usually it pleased her to be addressed as 'Madam' in court. But this old boy reminded her too much of a camp shop assistant for it to please her now.

Every witness was first obliged to produce a passport as proof of identity. When the old boy had handed his to the barrister and the barrister had risen and passed it on, Maddy riffled through its pages. In addition to the usual formality of checking his identity, she was doing what the Home Office had suggested that she do. Unfortunately the passport was a new one, less than five months old. It recorded only a single journey. But she was happy with that single journey. She pounced. 'Why did you spend three months in Tunisia?'

'Three months?' The watery eyes blinked at her. 'I'm sorry, madam…'

'It says here – three months. Three months,' she repeated. She tapped the right-hand page open before her with a fingernail.

'Oh, I think you're mistaken, madam. I spent only a week in Tunisia.'

'A *week?* Then why does it say— ?'

'I think, madam, that you'll find that that stamp is the visa stamp.' That he corrected her with such humility exasperated her far more than if he had been indignant or triumphant.

'A visa stamp?'

'Yes, madam, the Tunisians, er, give visas for a minimum of three months. One can also get them for, er, six months and even a year, I believe. But then one pays more. Naturally one pays more.' He gave a little cough, raising one hand to his mouth. 'I think, madam, that if you look on the opposite page you'll see the date stamps – arrival in Tunis, departure from Tunis.'

Maddy tossed the passport down on to her desk. Her face had flushed. He had made her look a fool and she did not care for that. But she had got him anyway, she consoled herself. He had been out of the country without the partner who, he had claimed in his statement in the bundle, was absolutely essential to his well-being.

Later in her examination of this pathetic creature (as she later referred to him when telling Jake of her day over dinner), she put it to him: 'So you rely a great deal on the appellant?'

'Oh, yes, madam. Yes. I couldn't manage without him. He's an exceptionally kind man. And efficient. When I was in hospital for an operation, a major operation, he spent the whole day by my bedside. Day after day. I kept urging him to go home but, no, he insisted. He even gave me a bath when I was well enough to get out of bed. He insisted on that. He wouldn't let the nurse do it.'

'I see.'

The trap had closed. Later she would write in her Reasons for Refusal: 'Mr L'Estrange maintained in his statement that he relied entirely on the appellant. This hardly accords with his visit, unaccompanied, to Tunisia for a holiday.' It was better not to specify that the period of the holiday had been only a week. Ideally, she would have liked to have been able to write 'a holiday of three months'.

At the close she said: 'Now, Mr L'Estrange, do you think that you can more precisely define for me the nature of your relationship with the appellant?'

He paused. Then, with unexpected boldness, he met her gaze and held it as he replied in a loud, firm voice: 'I love him. He loves me. That's the long and the short of it.'

'You are sure of that?'

'Absolutely.'

'I can understand your being sure about your own feelings. But how can you be sure about his?'

'We have now lived together for more than four years. He could not keep up a charade for that long.'

Muddy gave a small, pitying smile. It said: Oh, you self-deceiving fool!

'You're a retired dentist. Am I right?'

'That's right.'

'A distinguished dentist? You have a lot of letters after your name.'

'Oh, I don't know about that.' He smirked as he looked down at the long, folded hands that had been so skilful at dealing with expensive root-canal fillings and implants.

'Were some of the well-known people who wrote letters of support for you former patients of yours?'

'Yes. Yes, that is the case.' Intelligent enough to see what she was getting at, he hurriedly added: 'But they have all – well, most of them – met Mahmoud – er, my partner. They long ago came to regard me as a friend, and many, I think I'm right in saying, now also regard him as a friend.'

Again she gave that small, pitying smile.

'It is odd that there are no supporting letters from friends of his, in addition to those from these friends of yours.'

'My friends are his friends. He has no Moroccan friends now. He prefers it that way. In any case' – once again his voice surprised her by its loudness and firmness – 'would a recommendation from a fellow Moroccan carry much weight in a court of this kind?'

She paused, head lowered, as her nails still clicked over the keyboard. Then she looked up: 'Since you are retired, surely you could go to live in Morocco with the appellant? What's to prevent that, if you do not want to be separated?'

'Well...' He glanced first left, then right, as though for invisible support. 'I am an old man, eighty-one. My life is here. My friends are all here. I have lived in the same house for – let's see – yes, twenty-nine years. It's full of my books, my pictures, possessions. I have a bad heart condition. Cardiomyopathy. I see my specialist regularly. In Morocco I might not get the same standard of treatment. Might I? Then there are my two sisters. They are both widows. Both older than me. One is now in a nursing home. She's got senile dementia. One is – is here today. She is to be a witness. Her health is also bad. I like to think that I am a support to them – not just a financial support, in other ways too. I must be near them.'

'I see.' Again the nails tapped briskly on the keyboard. The she looked up. 'That will do.' The tone was curt. Other adjudicators said 'Thank you' to terminate an interview. 'Thank you' and 'please' were words that she herself preferred not to use when presiding in court. She believed strongly that, while in court, one had to show who was master. A lot of adjudicators – like that ass that she had replaced the day before - were far too eager to ingratiate themselves with appellants and their lawyers and witnesses.

The one-hour adjournment for lunch had ended. Maddy had eaten her sandwiches in the office with two of her female colleagues. The Moroccan and the old man and woman had found a café filled with workmen with dirty boots and loud voices and braying laughs.

The old woman now struggled to her feet. Her macintosh was draped over the back of the chair beside her and her beret, looking like a vast, hairy toadstool, lay on the seat. The barrister jumped up to help her, taking her left arm, the good one, even though it was with the hand of that one that the old woman was grasping her ferruled stick. 'Lean on me, dear,' she said not in her usual loud, gruff voice but in a liquid, cooing one. 'That's it.'

'I get giddy when I first get up. I'll be all right in a moment.'

'Take it easy! No hurry!'

'Since my stroke I tend to get this giddiness. After my first one I was fine, but since this one...'

'No hurry, no hurry!'

The barrister looked up at Maddy on the dais, in expectation of a sympathetic response. But Maddy was feeling far from sympathetic. She was asking herself: Is this, consciously or unconsciously, some kind of play-acting? Appellants often put on a performance. Only two or three weeks ago the fair-haired, pale-faced English wife of a Kosovan had arrived in court with a newborn baby in a pushchair, in order to be a witness. She had gazed adoringly at the Kosovan while rocking the baby in her arms. The court usher had later told Maddy that, on leaving the courthouse, the wife had got into one car with the baby, while the appellant had got into another, much larger one with two male friends. There had been the most perfunctory of goodbyes between husband and wife. The husband had paid absolutely no attention to the baby.

'I hope that I can hear properly,' the old woman said, having sat down. She appealed to the barrister: 'I wonder if you could just help me adjust my aid. It's difficult for me with my wonky arm.'

'Of course, dear.' It was said in the same liquid, cooing voice. 'What number do you want?'

'Could you turn it up to three? No, four might be better.'

Slowly, solicitously, the barrister began to take the old woman through the statement already presented in the bundle. Yes, Mr L'Estrange was her brother, her older brother. Yes, they had always been close. That was natural since her husband had been killed in the War, less than two years after he had married her. He had been a pilot, she added. Fighter Command. Yes, she had recently had the second of two strokes. That meant that she could no longer look after her little garden – or put out the rubbish – or lift the cat's tray. That sort of thing. Her brother and Mahmoud – his friend – were wonderful in that respect. She had only to ring them. It was Mahmoud of course who usually did all these little jobs. Her brother now had that heart problem.

The barrister leaned forward: 'Could you say something about the nature of the relationship between your brother and his – his friend?'

Briefly the old woman looked non-plussed. She pursed her lips, put a hand to her paralysed cheek, sighed. Maddy also now leaned forward. She was feeling a cynical amusement and also, yes, a cynical admiration. She often felt those emotions when listening to witnesses.

'It's not the sort of relationship that I ever knew much about until he – Mahmoud – came on the scene. I think my brother met him in some pub. There was the difference of age, a big difference. And there was the difference of interests. I don't want to sound snobbish in any way, but my brother is – well – well, he has no financial worries, none at all. And he's had a good education, loves books, opera, is interested in archaeology. Mahmoud is – different. He's an excellent sportsman. When not working in the restaurant, he spends most of his time playing football with a team on Highgate Heath or watching television. One has to accept that. But Mahmoud has made my brother happy. My brother's wife died five or six years ago – they had no children – and my brother then seemed to go into some kind of decline. He was horribly depressed. He stopped going out, entertaining. But now, with Mahmoud, he is happy. Happier than I've ever known him, I think – even during his marriage. They love each other – yes, they love each other. I'm sure they love each other. At first that seemed odd to me – even – yes – even rather shocking. But now ... Oh, I think it wonderful that they've found each other. It would be cruel if they had to separate. Terribly cruel.'

'If he went to live in Morocco, as has been suggested, how would that affect you?'

'Oh, I'd be absolutely devastated. Devastated. I don't know how I'd manage without all the support I get from him. And from Mahmoud too. They're wonderful to me, both of them, as I said.'

She broke off, looked fearfully up at Maddy, then pulled a handkerchief out of the pocket of her jacket and put it to one eye and then the other.

Suddenly, astonished, Maddy realised that all this rigmarole – as she had first thought of it – had moved her. No, it wasn't a rigmarole, it wasn't play-acting. It was as though she had listened to a thrush pouring out its valiant, artless song at the fall of a winter's night. It was *real*, just as the tears had been real. Her fingers suddenly stopped clicking at the laptop. Then she forced them to go on with their task of transcribing this banal and yet patently sincere witness to the reality of the love between an ancient, well-to-do, highly educated man and a young, impoverished, half-educated one.

'How do your family feel about the partnership?' the barrister prompted.

'Oh, we all accept Mahmoud as one of us. He comes to all our family gatherings – the Christmas dinners with my son and his wife and all the grandchildren – the weddings, the christenings. He even comes to the funerals!' She gave a little laugh. 'We all – all treasure him, you know. Even my little dog, my pug, treasures him. If I'm off colour Mahmoud travels all the way to Kennington to take Suzie for walks. And Arabs are not supposed to like dogs, are they?'

When the old woman had finished her testimony, Maddy astonished the barrister by saying 'Thank you', giving her first smile of the day, and not herself putting a single question or challenge.

'That brings our session to a close.' Maddy closed the laptop and put it under her arm. 'You will have my decision in the next four to six weeks.' She got to her feet.

'Was I all right?'

As Maddy left the room, she heard the old woman ask the barrister the question. She did not hear the answer.

In the office, Maddy refused the offer of a cup of coffee from the adjudicator whose place she had taken the day before. Inexplicably she had all at once begun to feel depleted and depressed. 'I must pick up the twins,' she told him. 'I'm already late for them.'

Thank God, the Volvo was there in the forecourt. But where on earth could Jake have taken it? One side was splashed with mud. On a closer inspection, she also saw that the roof was spattered with greyish-green bird shit. The interior reeked of cigarette smoke. He knew that she hated it when he smoked in the confined space of the car or of either of the two lavatories. Oh, it really was too bad!

As she drove off, she began to formulate what she would say in her report. As always the words leapt one after another into her nimble mind. *I do not accept that this Appellant holds a genuine belief that he will be persecuted or ill-treated were he returned to Morocco. His evidence was often confused and he repeatedly contradicted himself even when being questioned by his own counsel... It is perfectly credible that Mr L'Estrange is genuinely attached to the Appellant. But of the Appellant's attachment to Mr L'Estrange one might be forgiven for being more than a little cynical. After all...*

At that moment the words, previously jostling each other as they rushed out, tripped over each other, floundered, collapsed. That was what she ought to say, what *they* wanted her to say. But was it really what she felt? Was it the truth? Halted at the next traffic lights, she picked at the skin round the nail of her forefinger, then raised the forefinger to her mouth and tore at the tag of skin with her teeth. She felt the blood oozing out.

Soon after that, she saw the three figures walking through the rain sheeting down, inexorably malevolent. The L'Estrange man was a little ahead of the others. He was now using his sister's stick as he hobbled along. The Moroccan was carrying the old woman's handbag in one hand while with the other he held over her head a small, green, folding umbrella, presumably hers. Her good hand rested on his raised arm, even though that must have been uncomfortable for her, since he was so much taller than she was. Bowed, from time to time stumbling, she looked pitifully tiny and vulnerable. Clearly they had given up on the bus and were walking to the underground station. Maddy slowed, all but stopped. *Would you care for a lift...?* Those were the words that now leapt into her mind. Then she swept them out of it. It was no good to be sentimental about the spectacle of two old people and a young man battling against the rain as they trudge to an underground station. After all, the brother could have certainly afforded a taxi or a minicab. In any case, *they* had been right. One of them had said 'There are a lot of bad eggs and we have to smash them before they hatch out. If from time to time a good egg gets smashed in the process, well, in the interest of the safety of this country that's how it has to be.' He had gone on to talk of sleepers. 'All too often the more respectable these people seem to be, the more likely it is that they are up to something sinister.'

Could that handsome, fleshy Moroccan be up to something sinister? Why not? How would that pathetic, credulous couple know if he were?

She pressed the accelerator. Other words began to leap into her mind. *The Appellant has failed to discharge the burden upon him to the standard or at all...*

The school door was closed. The place, usually so noisy with its host of young children, was eerie in its silence. Maddy pressed the bell and then, her impatience getting the better of her, pressed it again only a few seconds later.

Miss Middleton's flat, cheery face appeared round the door. 'Oh, it's you. That wretched court must have kept you again!'

'Yes, I'm done in. I don't know how long I can go on with that job.'

'It must be your public spirit that holds you to it. The little ones are ready. Waiting.' She turned: 'Lucy! Laurel!   '

Suddenly the seven-year-old twins materialised on the upper landing of the grandiose staircase of the Edwardian house. They were wearing identical shiny black strap shoes, identical tartan skirts, and identical braces over their teeth.

Maddy held out both arms to them, as she cried out: 'The Campbells are coming!' It was something that she often cried out. Although born and bred in London, she was proud of her Campbell ancestry. 'But the Campbells are sorry they've come so late.'

'Oh, mummy, mummy!' They screamed in unison as they raced down the stairs and into her arms. Simultaneously Lucy said 'What happened to you?' and Laurel 'We've been waiting an age.'

'Sorry, darlings, sorry, sorry! Mummy had a horrible day. It began with Daddy forgetting to fill the petrol tank and then got worse and worse from then on. Never mind! The Campbells have come – at last, at long last. Oh, I'm so happy to be with my darlings!'

Everybody is Nobody

A few days before his death, Lois's 82-year-old father had remarked with wry melancholy: 'The old become invisible'. Now she herself had become invisible at the age of only thirty-seven. 'I'm here, here!' she wanted to shout across a road or down the aisle of a supermarket. 'Look at me!' But no one would look spontaneously, only when forced by her to do so. As someone whom she knew approached from a distance, she would become aware of the head wavering and the eyes swivelling away from her, to be followed by an abrupt scuttle across the road, even in the face of heavy traffic, or of a dart into a shop or down a side-turning.

It was not hostility, she constantly told herself. At first those with whom she and Brian came into even the most fleeting contact had been so sympathetic and helpful – their manner all too often suggesting that they themselves were drooping under the burden of the same intolerable grief as they were. Strangers had left flowers not merely at the house but, so it was reported, on the bank of that wide, calm, implacable river. By that river someone had even propped against a tree a Barbie doll, oppressively still in its box, its ever-open, thick-lashed eyes staring out through shiny cellophane. One ungainly mare of a woman, known only from the school run, had galloped towards Lois as they had simultaneously approached a letter-box, had thrown her arms round her and cried out 'Oh, oh, oh! I can't bear it.' It might have been she to whom the terrible thing had happened. But those times were over. Now there was only an

83

embarrassment so acute that people could no longer cope with it. Clearly they had decided, however unconsciously, that it would be better, if also brutal, to pretend that Lois had travelled out of their lives into a remote tundra of grief where it would be futile to try to reach her.

'It's not only that we might not exist,' Lois said to Brian. 'Poor little Suzie might never have existed.'

He stared at her with a desperate intensity. At work, he too had sensed that people once so matey now avoided his company, if they possibly could do so. 'Hello, Brian. How are things? Everything okay?' Then they hurried on, without waiting for the answer. How could everything be okay? His whole large, firm body would throb with rage against them for the idiocy of it.

'But she did exist,' he now said. 'We must never forget that.'

'Of course I never forget it! And never will! Sometimes — it's so odd — I feel that she *still* exists. Something rouses me in the middle of the night — just as she would sometimes rouse me when she'd had a nightmare. Of course I can't *see* her — never. But I think — I really think for a moment — yes, she's with us.'

'Why don't you wake me?'

She did not answer. Then at last she mumbled: 'Well, you need your sleep.'

He went across to the chair where she was seated, knelt before her, and took both her hands in his. He looked up imploringly at her with his wide-spaced, pale-blue eyes.

She jerked her head aside. 'Why does that bloody enquiry take so long? Why don't they *do* something?'

'These things always take time.' But he too constantly simmered with an inner fury at the delays. 'Those two wretches have both been suspended. They have to wait, we have to wait.'

Later that night, when he was snoring beside her, she awoke and peered, half in hope and half in apprehension, around the room. But no, on this occasion — unlike those many occasions before it — she received no sense of Suzie's presence. She did not know whether to be disappointed or relieved.

Slowly, as quietly as possible so as not to rouse him, she clambered out of the high bed and crossed over to the door. Its handle felt cold on her palm.

The boards creaked under her bare feet as, one hand to the wall, she made her way down the corridor. She often came into this room when Brian was at work and she was alone. If he knew that she had done so or was about to do so, he would chide her with a mixture of shared sorrow, love and exasperation – 'It's no good, love. Useless. It only makes things worse.'

'I suppose you think we ought to forget her? Oh, I so much want her back! It's all I want!'

He made no answer. No answer was possible.

She went into the narrow room, lit by the huge disk of an autumn moon far out above the fields belonging to neighbours whom they would once often meet at the pub or in each other's homes but whom they now rarely saw. She sat down on the bed. She pressed her hands together between her knees and bit on her lower lip. 'Come! Come! Oh, come back to us, Suzie!' Her whole being said it, a silent entreaty. Briefly a shadow seemed to flicker between her body, tense with supplication, and the extravagant moonlight. She almost thought that she heard a laugh, high, bell-like. Frantically, she turned her head from side to side. Then the moment had passed. She was alone, with the motionless, mute dolls and animals still ranged on the shelf that ran along the length of the bed. She felt suffocated by the silence and her solitariness. She gasped for breath. It was as if she herself were drowning in that river, her saturated clothes pulling her down, down, down, however frantically she struggled.

'I think they've forgotten us. They not only don't notice us, they've forgotten us.'

'These things all take time,' he said wearily. 'That's how the system works.'

'Fuck the system! At first the police were all soft voices and concern. Now we never hear a word from them. Was it – was it all pretending? And it's the same with Mr Bodley. For a few days – until the funeral was over … D'you remember how he said on television that this was a tragedy that no one connected with the school would ever forget? Well, he's forgotten bloody quick, and so have the rest of them.'

'People have to get on with their lives. He has a school to run. The police have crimes to solve.' He sighed. 'It's understandable.' But secretly, against all reason, he shared her indignation and rage. He too wanted to shout out: 'Pay attention to us! Don't forget us! Notice us! For God's sake notice us!'

★

Without telling him, Lois decided to return to the river. She could not drive there because, now that she no longer had the school run to make, Brian took the car to get to the office instead of travelling there by the bus. As she walked the two miles or so to the station, a car passed her and she saw that it was Dotty Lawson's cumbrous, ancient, dusty Volvo. There were three children in it, two of them Dotty's own tall, serene daughters and one a diminutive, fidgety boy belonging to some newcomers to the village. Once Suzie would also have been in the car, since Dotty and Lois had taken it in turns to do the school run. Now that boy had supplanted her. From time to time, unbidden and at once repudiated in horror, the thought would insinuate itself into her consciousness: Why couldn't that pathetic shrimp of a creature have drowned on that school excursion, instead of little Suzie? Everyone was always saying that it was a scandal how, grubby and dishevelled, he was all too clearly neglected by parents with high-powered jobs in television.

Lois wondered briefly if Dotty would stop to offer a lift or at least blow her horn or wave in greeting. But she drove implacably on, without even a momentary slackening of speed. *She must have seen me. She must have.* Dotty's two daughters, like so many of the other pupils, had come with their parents to the funeral. The younger of the two, along with some other of the girls, had sobbed noisily, her hand cupped over her mouth and nose as though she feared that she was about to vomit out her grief. That had been less than three months ago. It might have been years.

Well, at least the woman slumped opposite on the sparsely occupied train, noticed her. 'What a lovely day!' she remarked, smiling as a podgy hand tucked the errant front of her *broderie anglaise* blouse back inside the loosely woven tweed skirt that bulged over her protruding stomach. Was she pregnant, Lois wondered. Lois often thought of pregnancy for herself, as people think of suicide, with a mixture of dread and the feeling that it might put an end to an intolerable situation. Did she really want to have another child, as Brian so often urged? No, no! Such an attempt to replace the irreplaceable would be a betrayal of Suzie. Why couldn't he understand that? 'Yes, it is lovely,' she agreed with the woman, polite from habit.

The woman continued to make desultory conversation. She offered Lois her *Daily Mail* – she'd finished with it, she said. She even offered a sandwich. Then, discouraged by the two curt refusals and bare acknowledgement of this or that friendly remark, she gave up and stared out of the window instead.

The path down to the riverside was treacherous with a mulch of sodden leaves. At one point, as the recently fallen rain dripped off the bare branches of the trees on to the back of her lowered head, she slithered on a piece of abandoned cling-film and saved herself only by clutching at a tree-trunk. The tree-trunk left a greenish-grey stain on her palm. No one was about, either on the path or, when she finally reached it, on the curve of the riverbank, its grass glistening with what to her seemed a repellently metallic sheen. When she and Brian had last come here, there had been a number of anoraked anglers perched on canvas stools, isolated from each other and seemingly totally unaware of the woman who was sobbing violently, her face pressed into her companion's chest, while his arms encircled her.

She ventured towards the rickety jetty. The police thought that Suzie must have walked out along it, bent over to peer at something – perhaps that fish briefly glimpsed over there, Lois now thought, perhaps that Fanta bottle – and then slipped or lost her balance. Might someone have pushed her? It was Brian who had voiced that suspicion. The police thought not. There was no sign of assault, a willowy policeman had said. No sign of assault of any kind, the stout policewoman with him had confirmed. She had made a point of adding the last three words, even emphasising them, having intuited that Lois had speculated, in ever spiralling anguish, that before the drowning her beloved only child had been sexually assaulted.

Once again Lois asked herself: Oh, why, why had Suzie wandered off so far from the others? Had they been bullying her? Had those two wretched teachers, lovers she suspected, the woman with those huge, woebegone, dark-rimmed eyes, the man with those finicky gestures and those sudden pursings of his lips, said something to upset her? She had always been not merely an independent, but also an extremely secretive child. Now she had taken her last secret to the grave.

She stared out across the oily, almost motionless expanse of water. I could kill those two, she thought. Yes, lovers. Too much taken up with each other to notice what the children were doing. Criminals. Monsters. The sudden intensity of her hatred almost choked her. Desperately she looked around her for another human presence. She saw the black smudge of a crow high up in a dripping tree. Far off a dog was barking, but it was out of sight. The fish that she had seen before, or another fish like it, wriggled up briefly, a glinting silver dagger, then was lost in the murk of the water round the jetty.

In the train she stared out of the window as the light faded over the countryside unravelling beside her. Now there was no passenger opposite to attempt to lure her into banal conversation. At first she was glad of that, then she began to wish that there was someone, anyone.

Suddenly she thought of Suzie and the squirrel. For some unfathomable reason that spring the garden had pullulated with squirrels, as it had never done before. Most of them, whisking about the lawn or from branch to branch of the chestnut trees beyond it, would cautiously sidle towards the girl as she no less cautiously edged towards them, gazing intently at them while holding out some unshelled peanuts on a palm. Stooping now, the palm still outstretched, she would furiously will one of them to approach near enough to take one of the offerings. But only the smallest ever did so. That it was the same one on each occasion, she knew because down one of its sides it had a long, purple scar, an indentation in its otherwise luxuriant fur. Lois said that it must have been attacked by a dog, a cat or even a fox and then somehow escaped. This squirrel became for Suzie 'my squirrel'. Having assumed from the first that it was male, she had soon come to refer to it and even address it as 'Mr Squirrel'. Delicately, nose twitching, it would lower its head to her outstretched palm, open its mouth to show its small, murderously incisive teeth, and then would remove its prize and skip away with it. After that, she would scatter the rest of the peanuts for the others.

Then one day, for no apparent reason, instead of taking the nut in its jaws, it bit deep into the cushion of flesh below her thumb, and hung on there, its plump body twisting from side to side as though in a demonic frenzy, before racing off to the nearest tree and shooting up it. For a few seconds Suzie had suffered the attack in silence. Then she had let out a single piercing scream, which had brought Lois racing out from the kitchen to see what had happened. A series of gulping wails followed the scream.

The doctor had insisted on a tetanus injection, since the wound was deep. On the way home from his surgery, Suzie kept putting the lacerated hand over her mouth as though to suck at the wound under its dressing.

'Why did he do that? I don't understand. I've always loved him. I was feeding him. What happened?'

It was a mystery that defied explanation.

Repeatedly Suzie would revert to the subject. 'I was doing nothing to harm him. Nothing to hurt him. Why, mummy, why?'

She was a child who had never done anything in her life to hurt anybody. Her nature, as everyone remarked, was sweet, placid, caring. In no way had she deserved that bite so deep that it needed stitching. In no way had she deserved that terrible accident, alone and unnoticed, on the rotting jetty.

They approached each other, Dotty on one side of the street and Lois on the other. Now she'll pretend not to notice me, Lois thought. She'll turn her head to look up at those roses clambering over that wall, or she'll scuttle down that alley to the library. But to her amazement Dotty waved the newspaper that she was carrying and shouted 'Lois! Lois! I was coming over to see you.'

Lois halted and waited.

Dotty raced across the road, causing an oncoming van to hoot, brake violently and swerve. 'Have you seen this?' Now she was brandishing the paper.

'No. What is it?'

The paper was the free local one, pushed through the letter-box by an elderly woman piloting her load in what looked like a laundry basket on a rickety trolley. Lois and Brian always at once consigned the rag, unread, to the dustbin.

'It's about the plan for the school celebrations.'

'Celebrations? What celebrations?'

'The hundredth anniversary. You know. It's just coming up.'

'Celebrations?' At first Lois was merely stunned. 'But how can they be celebrating…'

'That's what I thought, How can they celebrate *anything* after the tragedy of poor little Suzie's…? I mean we've not even had the result of the enquiry. Those two are still suspended. As soon as I saw the item, I hurried over to show it to you.' Dotty was someone who enjoyed being indignant. She was constantly working herself up over grass verges left uncut, cars illegally parked, teenagers fooling about, noise, litter, vandalism.

89

'It's disgusting! How could they, how could they?' Lois was no longer merely stunned. All at once she was shaking with fury.

Dotty was delighted with this reaction. 'What can we do about it?'

'I'll speak to Brian.'

'We must do something. They say here' – she shook the paper – 'that Princess Anne is going to come. Can you imagine?'

But Dotty's indignation had a way of flaring up briefly and then guttering out. It did so on this occasion. 'Getting worked up is like an orgasm for her,' Brian remarked bitterly. 'Lots of frantic threshing about for a short time. Then it's all over and she drifts off.' Dotty said that she'd spoken to, oh, lots and lots of people. They'd all agreed that it was a disgrace, an absolute disgrace. But would they do anything about it? No, of course not. Typical! It was the same over those new school uniforms. Everyone loathed them but no one, not a single bloody parent – except, of course, herself – had had the guts to put a head above the parapet. 'I'm sorry, darlings, I'm truly sorry. My heart bleeds for you. Sometimes I can't sleep for brooding on what you two are going through.'

As the day of the commemorations approached, the usually lethargic little community was galvanised. Lois and Brian tried to ignore what news filtered through to them of the sports events, the concert and the pageant tracing the history of the school. When they received an invitation to attend, Lois at once tore it into shreds. Would the two suspended teachers be allowed to be present? 'I shouldn't be surprised.' Brian replied bitterly. 'Perhaps that bitch has directed the play,' Lois said. 'She's always been the one in charge of drama.' They experienced a brief moment of satisfaction when they heard that Princess Anne would not, after all, be able to attend. But soon after it was proclaimed that Princess Michael of Kent would do so.

Suddenly, on the day before the celebrations, Brian had his idea. Having come home early from his office, he at once set to work on the materials that he had brought back with him in the car. Lois stood over him, watching, arms folded. From time to time she nodded or said 'Yes. That's right. Yes, yes.' He would then look up and smile at her conspiratorially. It was the first time that they had felt happy since Suzie's death.

With a felt-tipped pen, tongue caught between his large, white teeth, he began to inscribe in huge capital letters:

LESS THAN ELEVEN WEEKS AGO, OWING TO INEXCUSABLE NEGLIGENCE OF
TWO MEMBERS OF THE STAFF OF THIS SCHOOL, A LITTLE GIRL LOST HER
LIFE. AS HER PARENTS WE PROTEST. IS THIS THE TIME TO HAVE A
CELEBRATION?

He turned his head up towards Lois. 'All right?'
She nodded.
'Sure? You don't think we should add anything?'
She shook her head. 'Best short. And sharp.'

A number of other people, mostly women and many of those with small
children in pushchairs, were already waiting to see the Princess. Brian,
with Lois on his heels, ruthlessly used his placard to, in effect, beat a way
to the front. Caught in his slipstream, one diminutive boy almost toppled
over and began to wail. 'Would you mind?' a woman whom Brian had
inadvertently jostled and then banged, protested angrily.

Brian hoisted the placard high over his head. But curiously,
infuriatingly, no one seemed to want to look at it, let alone read it. In the
crowd were people whom he and Lois immediately recognised – that
nice, fat girl who was always so helpful at the Sainsbury's cake counter, the
postman whose asthma attacks made his deliveries so erratic, the mother
of that little French girl whom Suzie had invited to her last birthday party
– but, by now predictably, not one gave any indication of recognising
them in return.

Eventually Lois swivelled round to face the Sainsbury's girl, who was
standing just behind her. 'Hello!' she said. She forced a smile, which
unfortunately raised the left side of her mouth in what might have been
mistaken for a snarl.

The girl gave a little bob, as though rehearsing a curtsey for the Princess,
and smiled back nervously. 'Hi!' At that, she turned away and sidled off.

The Princess was late. When the ancient Rolls Royce, accompanied
by four outriders on motorcycles and two police cars, one behind and one
in front, at last came into view, there was some desultory clapping.
Revealed through the bullet-proof window was a middle-aged woman in
a shiny, pale-blue dress and a dark-blue felt hat the large brim of which
swept upwards and away from her face. With marionette-like movements,
she smiled, nodded, waved a hand, leaned forward, smiled again.

91

'She looks even better in real life than in her photographs,' a woman beside Lois remarked to another woman.'

'Pity the make-up's so thick,' the other woman responded.

The child beside her asked: 'Mummy, who's that lady?'

'It's the Princess, you little silly!'

Brian was still holding the placard aloft with aching arms. He now tried to step out in front of the stately, hearse-like vehicle to brandish it before the graciously smiling face framed by the window. But a policeman put out a hand. 'Stand back, sir! Please, sir! Stand back!'

The Princess continued to nod, smile, wave, nod. But, mysteriously, she never looked at the placard, even though it was so close to her, at the front of the crowd.

Silently, slowly, the Rolls Royce glided on and eventually passed through the high wrought-iron gates.

'She didn't even notice!' Lois cried out. 'I can't believe it. I just can't believe it.'

Later, as she and Brian trailed home together, he at last broke their despairing silence: 'You'd have thought that at least that press photographer would have taken a shot. What's the matter with people?'

'What's the matter with them? They're all heartless shits.'

He flung the placard away from him on to the grass verge. 'It's disgusting, disgusting, *disgusting*!' he cried out. He might have been a bewildered and frustrated small boy.

There were people all around them. But again no one paid any notice.

Every Sunday they drove out to the cemetery. Recently extended, it now also included a crematorium, a Garden of Rest full of meticulously tended hybrid roses, and a café at which luke-warm coffee and tea were served in plastic mugs and the sandwiches tasted of the polythene in which they had been wrapped.

'Why are there so many people here today? It's not usually like this.'

'Easter,' Brian replied. Despite his thick, dark-blue overcoat, black cap and black gloves, he felt chilled. It was all he could do to stop his teeth from chattering.

'What has that to do with it?'

'Well, the Resurrection, I suppose.'

'Yes, of course.' Oddly, though Lois believed in a resurrection for Suzie, she had never been able to believe in one for others or for herself.

They had brought with them, in a Safeway's bag carried by Brian, half-a-dozen pots of primroses, a trowel, a fork, and a dustpan and brush. They knelt on either side of the grave and silently got to work. Brian planted the primroses, Lois swept up the sodden leaves and small twigs that the March winds had blown across from the rowan tree beside the grave. She was superstitious about rowans, as about many other things. It was a comfort that it was there. Weren't rowans supposed to ward off evil spirits?

It was, surprisingly, Brian, always so down-to-earth, and not Lois, often so sentimental, who had composed what should go on the newly cut tombstone. When she had been in the cemetery for the burial of a neighbour, Dotty had happened to pass the tombstone, had paused to read the inscription, and had then remarked to her husband, a chartered surveyor, 'Rather naff, don't you think?'

The inscription read:

IN MEMORY OF OUR ANGEL SUZIE
HER WINGS WERE STILL SMALL
BUT STRONG ENOUGH TO BEAR HER TO HEAVEN

Now Lois used the brush meticulously to coax every residue of dust and grime out of each of the incised letters. Then, with a cloth, she rubbed at them with energetic fury.

Across the narrow path, a middle-aged woman with improbably fox-coloured hair and a knitted coat reaching almost to her swollen ankles, and an elderly man with a straggly white moustache, were putting some flowers into a glass vase, which the woman had already filled from a tap at the entrance gate. There was a look of resigned sorrow on both their faces.

Suddenly the woman lurched up from her kneeling position on a newspaper that she must have brought with her, and approached Lois and Brian. 'That's a lovely rose you have there. I wanted a rose like that. White, with small buds like those. But the man at Cassell's must have made a mistake. What we got came up with some of the largest of red roses either of us had ever seen. You can imagine! Once it produced its first flower, we decided it wasn't suitable. Not for a grave. Not at all. My mother would have been horrified. So we transplanted it to our little garden. But —' she shrugged mournfully — 'it just died.'

'We felt our rose bush was just right for our little daughter,' Lois said. 'Those white buds. Just right. She was so young when she was taken from us. Those small white buds express her so perfectly.'

Now the woman had been joined by her husband. With a Welsh lilt to his voice, he said: 'It's her mother who rests over there. The wife and her mother were always so close. She was a lovely lady. A really lovely lady. We never had a cross word. She was a dinner-lady at the local school for almost thirty years. The kids loved her.'

'Which school was that?' Brian asked. 'Perhaps it was the one to which my little daughter went.'

Neither answered the question. 'My mother won a George medal,' the woman took up. 'In the War. She was working in a canteen in London at the time and it was bombed. She helped rescue a lot of people. She was a strong woman, always strong. Afraid of nothing.'

'Our little one didn't know what fear was,' Brian said. 'We think that may be why she died as she did. She may have strayed away from the school party and then...'

The woman cut in: 'When I was little, my mother had this wonderful hair. Golden. It was so long she could sit on it. Then my father persuaded her to cut it off. I cried and cried and cried. It was the worst day of my life.'

'We must get our skates on, Marion. Don't forget Elsie said she'd come by at six.'

'Yes, that's right.' The woman turned away, then turned back. 'Oh, I miss my mother so much. Not a day passes that I don't think of her. She was one of the old school, you know. She had her principles and she stuck to them.'

Without a word of goodbye, the man hurried back to the other grave and began to pick up the thing scattered around it.

'Well, it's been nice talking to you.' A perfunctory, twitchy smile. Then the woman too had left them.

Lois and Brian completed their tasks in silence. Then they got to their feet. Brian bent down to brush his trousers. Lois held a handkerchief to lips chapped by the March winds, as though she were about to cry. The two of them stood there in silence for a long time, their heads lowered. Then Brian sighed: 'Well, I suppose we'd better be getting home.'

'I always think – it's terrible that she – she can't come home with us.'

He put his arm round her. 'I know, I know.' He felt the same coldness and immensity of grief. But, unlike her, he rarely attempted to put that grief into words.

Lois thought of the isolation of bereavement, as she often did. Here were all these people, dotted around the cemetery. But each little group was totally uninterested in any other little group. No one noticed anybody, she thought. Each group was invisible to the rest. She tried to catch the eye of a woman standing alone by a grave that they passed. But at that same moment the woman turned away, stooped, and tugged at a weed.

Without looking at Brian, almost to herself, Lois said in a low, mournful voice: 'Everybody is somebody. But to everyone else everybody is nobody.'

Brian made no response. The two of them trudged on.

Then Brian shivered. 'I'm chilled to the bone,' he said. 'Let's go to the caff and have a cup of tea.'

'You're optimistic if you think that that dishwater of theirs is going to warm us.'

Nonetheless they branched off along the path that would take them there.

The Miracle

For the Ukraine cruise I had a single cabin on a lower deck. Sonny and Joy, as befitted a couple so rich, had one of the four 'stateroom suites' on the boat-deck, each with its own private area for sunbathing. It was to this area that the three of us increasingly retreated, when not ashore. Joy, always a serene, remote presence, would work at her embroidery or would read some work of historical biography. Sonny would talk about the arts, politics or life in general, with the same showy bravura, all too often based on inadequate knowledge or total ignorance, with which he used once to dash off his weekly essays when, both reading English, we had shared a tutor at Oxford. When the ship was docked, it was from this eyrie that we invariably used to look down all the activity below us.

A pall of smog, leaden and acrid, hung over Zaporizhzhya. We had moored opposite a long, narrow beach, in effect a mudflat, crowded with bathers. I could taste the smog on my tongue; it made me wheeze with the asthma from which I had until then been mercifully free on the trip.

'Who wants to visit the "Cradle of Cossackdom"?' Sonny asked, contemptuously quoting from our programme.

'What else is there to do?' Joy asked.

'Read. Talk. ... Drink,' he added. The last was something that he had been doing increasingly during the past week.

All but a few of the other passengers set off in antiquated buses for the Cossacks' island; but after a brief protest from Joy, the three of us remained behind, lying out on deckchairs in our privileged space. An ice bucket glinted beside Sonny.

Just as I was about to drop off to sleep, a cooling wind arose to pick away at the pall of smog, until everything was radiant – the brass of the ship glowing, the sea glittering with shards of light, the sky a lucent blue. We began to look down at the youthful people, a few girls among them but chiefly boys, who were diving into the dirty water both from the quay at which our boat was moored and from a suspension bridge that led from the quay across the wide, meandering river to the beach.

'You'd think they'd get typhoid,' Joy said to me.

'We certainly would if we dived into that muck.'

Sonny picked up his Japanese video camera – one of our fellow passengers, a retired solicitor, had remarked to me, with sour envy, that it must be one of the most expensive on the market – and leaned over the rail, filming now one of the divers and now another. Eventually, the divers became aware of what he was doing and they began to vie with each other, climbing higher and higher up the arch of the suspension bridge, before daringly plunging into water iridescent with oil and murky with garbage. 'Such beauty in such a hideous place,' Sonny muttered, as a tall girl with hair bleached by the sun almost to white, gazed up at us, eventually to be joined by a squat boy with a simian face, short legs and swelling pectorals.

Eventually Sonny padded in his espadrilles into the stateroom and emerged with a half-full carton of the Camel cigarettes at which he puffed so frequently that his clipped moustache had an orange tinge to its grey. Now, when a diver performed a particularly graceful or courageous feat, he would lay aside the camera and hurl a packet of the cigarettes down to the quay. The divers always seemed to know for whom the reward was intended. There was, amazingly, no pushing or squabbling.

The squat boy with the simian face was the most accomplished performer. He could not have been more than thirteen or fourteen, but he was clearly a hero even to his older friends. When he had executed a particularly impressive dive, they would clap him, not with any irony but in genuine admiration, before Sonny threw down yet another packet of the Camels. The two guards who always stood watch by the gangway when we were in port, from time to time stared up at us. Were they scowling like that because of the glare or because they disapproved of, or were envious of, Sonny's largesse?

Having now dived off the highest point of the arch of the suspension bridge, to the cheers of his companions, the squat boy must have decided to find an even greater challenge. As though on an impulse, he raced along the quay and, with a flying leap, straddled the rail of the main deck. The guards rushed towards him but, with a yell of triumph, he eluded them by shinning up the side of the ship, finding a precarious foothold now here and now there, until he was on the next deck. He then raced up one companionway after another, until all at once he emerged, panting, on the boat-deck beside us. He ran towards one of the lifeboats, suspended from its davits over the murky water, and, teeth bared in a grin, jumped on to it. He stared across at us with what seemed to be a challenge. Sonny laid down the camera on the table on which the vodka bottle and glasses were set out and drew his wallet out of the back pocket of his linen trousers. He pulled out a fifty-dollar bill and held it aloft. He and the boy grinned at each other in mutual understanding. Sonny waved the bill back and forth. Then he handed it to me and stooped for the camera.

I could hear the two guards pounding up the companionway. They were shouting something, unintelligible to us but intelligible to the boy, who turned away, braced himself, prehensile toes gripping the edge of the boat, and, arms raised above his squat body, dived.

It would be a perfect dive, I remember thinking, thrilled, as always, by an athletic prowess beyond me even when young. But then it seemed as if some invisible, malevolent hand reached out and nudged the plunging body sideways – so that, instead of arrowing straight down into the murky waters, it veered at a slight angle and crashed on to the quay. Joy beside me screamed. Others, below us, also screamed.

'Oh, Christ!' It was like a bellow of pain from Sonny.

He met the first of the guards at the top of the companionway, pushed the man aside, and raced down.

Joy, as horrified as I was, placed a hand on my arm. 'Do you think ...?'

I shrugged helplessly. I thought for a moment that I was going to vomit . I had already decided that the boy must be dead.

The two of us stared down, as a crowd, composed not merely of the divers but of people from the beach and even from the road beyond it, grew larger and larger and more and more clamorous around the motionless, sprawled body on the jetty. Suddenly the ship's doctor – a retired Russian gynaecologist, with huge feet and a spade-shaped white, tangled beard – had appeared on the scene. Sonny gripped him by his arm, saying something to him. The doctor pushed Sonny aside, knelt by the boy, raised his arm and felt his pulse. The boy's face was unnaturally twisted askew, the one visible eye shut. Something dark and glistening was forming a triangular pool to one side of it.

'What a crazy thing to attempt!' I said to Joy.

'And Sonny egged him on. Oh, God! It was his fault. What an idiot!'

An ancient ambulance, bell jangling, eventually arrived, and two medics, a gaunt, middle-aged man and a young, busty woman, both in long, grubby white coats, hoisted the body on to a stretcher.

The doctor clambered into the ambulance and then turned to push aside the tall girl diver with the sun-bleached hair – she was hysterically sobbing – as she attempted to follow. To my amazement Sonny now also attempted to board the ambulance. The doctor barked something and Sonny, vigorously shaking his head, yelled something back. For a while, they argued. Then both disappeared into the ambulance. Bell again jangling, it jerked towards the bridge, bumped across it and gathered speed.

'What use does the fool think he will be?' Joy asked. Usually so placid, she amazed me with the tone, harsh with anger, with which she asked the question.

I shrugged. 'I suppose in some way he feels responsible.'

'Of course he feels responsible! He ought to feel responsible! If he hadn't encouraged that boy ... And now he's dead. That's clear. He's dead.' Suddenly she began to sob with a gulping, jerky frenzy. Then she rushed into the stateroom, leaving me alone. I went to the rail and stared down at the crowd. More and more of them began to stare up at me in still, silent hostility – as though it were I who had held out that fifty-dollar bribe.

When Sonny at last returned, I expected him to be shaken and shocked by the realisation that, however indirectly, he had been the cause of a death. When, to my amazement, he revealed that the boy was suffering from nothing worse than concussion and a shattered cheekbone, I expected him to show the jubilation of relief. What I never expected was his air of stupefied bewilderment. Frowning out at the by now deserted beach, across which the shadows of the straggly trees behind it were lengthening as the huge sun sank, he would answer each of our questions – Was the hospital far away? Would the shattered cheekbone require an operation? When did they think that the boy would come out of his coma? – with two or three tetchy words. It was as though he were trying to work out some difficult problem and did not wish to be interrupted. Eventually the gong reverberated tinnily for dinner. He picked up his glass of neat vodka – it must have been his fourth or fifth since his return – and said: 'You both go. I've no appetite.'

As we walked towards the dining-hall, Joy said: 'What a relief! He could never have lived with himself if the boy had died.'

'But it's so extraordinary. I felt sure that he must have broken his neck.'

The ship was to sail at midnight. Sonny and I walked along the deserted quay, until all at once I glimpsed that triangle of blood, now no longer luridly glistening but dried almost to black.

'I thought he was dead, I really thought he was dead.'

Sonny halted, turned to me. Although the night was cool and we had been merely ambling along, there were beads of sweat on his forehead. 'He *was* dead,' he said. 'That's what I don't understand. The doctor told me he was dead. He *was* dead.'

'That doctor never struck me as in the least bit competent.'

'He *was* dead.'

'Well, it was certainly a miracle that after a fall like that ... '

'Yes. Yes.' Again he halted, gripped my arm. 'A miracle. That was what it was.'

'As I looked down, I was willing him not to be dead – willing it, willing it!' I confessed. 'But I find that, when I will things, they never happen.'

He shook his head. 'I thought for a time that I was willing it too – as I sat beside him in the ambulance. But I wasn't. I was begging – entreating – someone that he shouldn't be dead. But whom was I begging – entreating? That's what's so strange. And who heard me? Who heard me? Who heard me and came up with that miracle?'

When – at Joy's, never Sonny's, invitation – I subsequently visited the vast, over-furnished house in Brompton Square, Sonny was rarely present. Either he had hidden himself away in his room or he had deliberately gone out to avoid me, I decided. Joy, embarrassed and anxious, would make some excuse – at the last minute he had had to take charge of a relative on a visit from the States, he had been detained by business in Paris, he had missed a train. On one occasion, ignoring whatever such excuse she had just come up with, I asked: 'Is something the matter with him?'

'Oh, no! No! He's – all right.' She was flustered and hesitant. Her face began to redden.

Eventually we lost touch with each other. Twice, at widely spaced intervals, Joy invited me round and, for perfectly legitimate reasons, I had to refuse. I stopped dropping in, as I once used sometimes to do if I had been shopping in the area. I did not invite them back. Friendships have a natural cycle that often ends in a withering away and then a total dissolution. Perhaps ruthlessly, I have always thought it pointless to keep them on a life-support system beyond their natural expiry date.

Last week at a dinner-party I found myself sitting opposite an elderly man whom, I remembered, I had met many years before at a typically lavish, rowdy cocktail party given by Sonny and Joy. He was Sonny's stockbroker. Inevitably I asked after the couple. 'Sonny now seems uninterested in all the things that interested him before,' he told me in his precise, metallic voice. 'Doesn't go to the theatre, doesn't play golf, doesn't go to parties, doesn't give parties. Doesn't hunt women, doesn't gamble. Can you imagine that? Sonny no longer chasing a skirt, Sonny no longer gambling. And only two or three years ago he was constantly in pursuit of someone or other, and would make or lose twenty grand at the tables in a night.'

'What do you think is the reason for the change?'

The man shrugged. 'I sometimes wonder if he hasn't had some sort of breakdown.' I stared at him in incredulity. Sonny had always seemed to me far too mentally and emotionally robust for a breakdown. 'People do, you know,' he said. 'The very rich far more often than the very poor. But – amazingly – he seems to be happy. As though he had received some wonderful news that he can't tell us about. So perhaps it isn't a nervous breakdown. Perhaps it's something else at which we can only guess. Who knows?'

I have just been for a walk in nearby Holland Park. There's an arbour there, with a long bench, where the winos congregate. Usually I try to avoid passing that way, because it embarrasses me when they shout out at me for money. Today, bunched together at one end of the bench, two disheveled, red-faced men were drinking from cans. On another bench not far distant, an old man with grey, untidy hair, in a rumpled suit and scuffed brogues, was slouched, swollen hands on knees and legs thrust out. He might have been mistaken for a wino himself. Eyes closed, he had uptilted his blotchy, heavily lined face to the sun. He was smiling, not at me or at anyone else, in beatific contentment.

It was Sonny. I paused, stared at him. His eyes remained closed, the smile broadened. Then feeling, I could not have said why, that he had entered a region where I, friends far closer, and perhaps even Joy could no longer follow, I hurried away.

The Sunlight on the Garden

In his tweed overcoat, a cap of the same brown-and-green tweed pulled down low over his forehead, Maurice Ransome sat out in his London garden. His gloved hands were clasped over the paunch that exercise and intermittent dieting were incapable of shifting. His red-rimmed, melancholy eyes were shielded from the glare by glasses that automatically darkened and lightened. These past days he had had the illusion that they were more often dark than light. He shivered. *The sunlight on the garden hardens and grows cold.* Where had that come from, a dead leaf eddying down into his consciousness? Auden? MacNiece? Spender? One of those, certainly. Strange how in old age one's memory functioned – or failed to function. For several minutes that morning he had been unable to remember his niece's married name when sending an Easter card in answer to her ridiculous one of a chicken hatching out of an egg (he was meticulous about such things); and yet that quotation, long shrivelled, was now suddenly pulsing with sap.

The telephone was ringing. His niece had given him a mobile but it lay in a drawer with other unused things like his dress-studs, his field-glasses and the dental plate that had had to be replaced with one that better fitted his shrinking gums. His body seemed to creak in protest as he staggered to his feet. With an effort, he straightened it. Then, a still impressive figure with his closely cropped white hair, white moustache and impressive arch of a nose, he marched into the house as though about to carry out a military inspection.

'Is that Sir Maurice Ransome?' It was a woman's voice, with a vestigial foreign accent. Romanian, he at once thought. He had always been good at accents, just as he had always been good at languages.

'That's right.' She must be one of those people who wanted to sell one double-glazing, interest one in some dodgy investment, or persuade one to give to a charity of which one had never heard. 'Yes? What is it you want?'

'You won't know who I am. I don't imagine you'll remember after all these years.'

'Well, tell me.'

'I'm the daughter of Denisa Popescu. You know who I mean?'

'Of course.'

'I'm Ana. Ana Williamson. The Williamson is the name of my ex.' She gave an embarrassed laugh. 'Long ago I heard that we were neighbours.'

'You heard? How did you hear?'

'Oh, someone told me. Maybe my mother. And then today – I don't know why – I looked in the telephone book and there I found your number. I thought you'd be ex-directory. But you weren't.'

'Is your mother with you?'

'No. No, she died two, three years ago. I thought you might have known.'

'No. No one told me. We had – lost touch. It's all so long ago, that stay of mine in Bucharest.'

'My mother said that you had once told her that it was the happiest time of your life.'

He had told many women that this or that time was the happiest. 'I was young. Well, comparatively young.'

'My mother told me never to get in touch with you.'

'I can't think why she told you that.'

A silence. Each waited for the other.

Then she said: 'It would be nice if we could meet?'

He wanted to say 'Why?' He wanted to say 'No, I don't really think so.' Then he relented: 'Yes. If you'd like that. Of course. Why not?'

That night he dreamed of Denisa. He had not thought of her for twenty and more years. They were trying to get into a museum, a towering Gothic building dripping with ivy, which was locked. She repeatedly rang the bell, she rattled a vast iron ring of a door handle, she banged with a fist. Then she snatched his hand and dragged him round the building to a side door. That too was locked. 'But they said someone would be here to open it for us,' she burst out. 'What's the matter with this country?'

What's the matter with this country? It was something that she had often cried out in frustration and fury.

He woke. The eiderdown had slipped off his bed. He was cold. Almost everything in those far-off days was wrong with the country. One of those things was Denisa herself – or, rather, her role. He had soon realised that, so fluent in English, so critical of the regime and so free in her comings and goings, she must be a plant. Later she even confessed it to him – 'I just report things of no importance. If I didn't report something, then I'd have to leave the job. And stop seeing you. You understand that, don't you?' Of course he understood it. He might have then sent her packing. But, alone in Romania because his wife did not think it a suitable place for an ailing child constantly requiring expert medical attention, he had needed Denisa.

As he shaved, with the cutthroat razor that, innately conservative, he still preferred, he wondered what Denisa's daughter would be like. *His* daughter too? He stared at his reflection in the glass, opened his eyes wide, slowly shook his head. He remembered how, after a day of ski-ing under a pale-blue, cloudless sky, she had told him, turning her head on the pillow and smiling: 'I have a surprise for you.'

When she had revealed to him the nature of the surprise, he had answered: 'And I have a surprise for you.'

'Yes?' There was a tinny note of apprehension in her voice.

'It's not something I like to talk about. But medically it's impossible I'm the father. Our child has a genetic disorder. Inherited from me. So – a few years ago I had an operation. A vasectomy. You know what that is? One didn't want to take a risk.' He often spoke of himself as 'one.'

After that he could not feel the same towards her, nor she towards him. But their affair continued until, a few weeks later, he moved on to another diplomatic posting. She never spoke again about the pregnancy during those weeks, but in the desultory correspondence that for a brief period had followed his departure, she had told him of the birth of a daughter and of her determination not to give her up for adoption, as her family had urged her to do.

★

'Let me carry that for you.'

'No, it's not really – '

'Please. Let me!'

'Oh, all right.'

She had already picked up the tray from the kitchen table.

'You have a beautiful garden.'

' Very small.'

'But beautiful.' Without being asked she began to pour out the tea.

'People – friends, busybody neighbours – keep telling me that I ought to have all these trees pruned. One gets so little sunlight.'

'I think they're right.'

'But I don't want more sunlight.'

'Maybe one day I'll do some pruning for you. I'm a good gardener. But now I live in an attic flat and so I have no garden. My ex has the garden now. It was our garden, now it's his.' The tone was humorous, without any bitterness. The pale blonde hairs on her strong forearms glistened in the afternoon sunlight. Suddenly he was pierced by a memory. It was of his mother lying out on a deckchair on the top deck of the Lloyd Triestino liner that brought them back home from India when he was a child. Pale blonde hairs glistened on her bare forearms. The child had put out a tentative hand and brushed the back of it against those hairs. At the contact, he had felt a shiver of delight.

He stared up at this woman who was deliberately cutting the chocolate cake, her lower lip drawn between her teeth as though she were concentrating on some difficult task. As soon as he had opened the door to her, he had been tantalised by a resemblance that he could not define. Now it had come to him: She looked like his mother – the same eyebrows, each at first a straight line and then a rising one, the same almost gaunt cheek-bones, the same uptilted nose with the slightly flared nostrils. But he was fancying that resemblance! She was in no way related to his mother. She was the daughter of Denisa and some lover of hers.

'I know nothing about you. First, tell me what you do.'

She was receptionist at a medical centre, she told him. It was, he realised, not far from his house; he had often passed it and had wondered whether he should not register there, since he was dissatisfied with repeatedly having to wait for an appointment at the one to which he went. The trouble was that she had no real qualifications, she said. Without qualifications it was difficult to get the sort of job she wanted – in publishing, in broadcasting. She had married at seventeen. She talked of the marriage, troubled and brief. A mistake, she said.

'And you? Do you live alone here?'

'Yes, since my wife died. That was four, no, five years ago. Time flies when one is old, one loses account of it.'

'You have a son. I remember my mother told me that.'

'*Had.* Died years and years ago.'

'You don't mind living alone?' She jumped up to refill his teacup.

'One gets used to it. In fact, in the end one rather prefers it. For a time after my wife's death a cousin of mine volunteered to come here as housekeeper. No good. Nothing wrong with her, decent woman, always kind, but it just didn't work. In the event, one had to make an excuse to end the agreement. Poor soul – the excuse didn't convince her, I'm afraid.'

She was looking round the garden. 'This lawn will never grow properly. Too much shade. Why not have it paved?'

'I like what grass there is.'

'York stone. That would be fine.'

He ignored it. He stared at her hands as they now rested one on either knee, as though preparatory to departure. They were beautiful hands, the nails carefully manicured, natural in colour as he liked nails to be.

When she was leaving, she said: 'I was serious about the garden. I'd love to put in some work on it.'

'I do have a chappie who comes in from time to time.'

'Why go to that expense? I'd do it for nothing.'

He watched her from his upstairs bedroom window as, mounted on a ladder, she sawed at a branch. Her hair, brown streaked with gold, was dishevelled about her shoulders, and there were patches of sweat, dark on light, staining the cotton of her blouse under the arms. Her energy and strength overwhelmed him. All around her were the severed branches of privet and cotoneaster. They looked almost black against the yellowish green of the long grass that she had said she would mow the coming day.

He went down and joined her. From the ladder, looking down at him, she said: 'Oh, I do wish you'd have that lawn paved. You could have two urns with flowers in them. You could even have a fountain. Oh, do!'

He shook his head, smiled. 'Nope. I like it as it is.'

'Oh, you are obstinate!'

'Yes. Yes, I am.' He laughed.

She spoke of the tenants below her. 'It's odd how noise rises. I hear that thump-thump-thump late into the night. When I last complained, he — the man — called me a fucking bitch and then slammed the door on me.' A few days later she spoke again of them. When they had their parties, they wedged the front door open. It was so dangerous, anyone could slip into the house. 'I'll just have to find somewhere else to live.'

Soon after that, he was in bed with a summer virus. He wheezed, coughed and expectorated, now sweating and now shivering. She had called round unexpectedly with two rosebushes and had stared at him, in his pyjamas and slippers, his forehead shiny with sweat, as he had opened the door to her. Then she was all concern. She demanded a thermometer, which he had difficulty in locating in a bedside drawer, and, having peered down at it, at once told him: 'You must get to bed. It's over a hundred.'

'Oh, one doesn't give in to a temperature. I feel fine.'

'You look ghastly.'

Eventually he gave in both to the temperature and to her with a feeling of voluptuous relief. She dosed him with aspirin, brought a bowl of chicken soup and a pot of yoghurt up to his room on a tray, and announced that, having gone home to see to one or two things, she would return to spend the night.

'Oh, but that's not at all necessary! One can manage perfectly well.'

Again she insisted. Then, so far from continuing to oppose her, he suddenly gave in. with an upsurge of joy that took him by surprise.

'I'm going to be terribly busy the next few days. I must do some house hunting.' She was cleaning the silver, some of it tarnished to almost black, that his daily, who was in fact a weekly, never had either the time or the inclination to tackle.

'So you're really set on a move?'

Vigorously she rubbed at the side of an entrée dish now rarely used. She nodded, her hair falling forward to screen her face. He wanted to put out a hand to feel the thickness of that hair, his fingers lifting up strands of it and then letting them fall over forearm and palm. 'What else can I do? Things can't go on as they are. I hardly slept a wink last night. And when I was coming up the steps behind him yesterday, he just shut the door in my face. Deliberately. No doubt about it.'

'He sounds an absolute little shit.'

'Not little. He's even taller than you are. And huge. He plays rugby in his spare time.' Again she rubbed vigorously. 'The trouble is that everything in this area's so expensive. Even a bed-sitter with its own kitchen and bathroom. I'll have to look farther afield. Someone said that Bow might be worth a try.'

'*Bow!*' He was appalled. 'But that's miles away.'

'Yes, I know. If I went there, I'd have to find another job. I couldn't make that long journey from Bow to Kensington each day.' The implication was obvious to him. She could not each day make that long journey from Bow to him.

'I have an idea.' He said it on an impulse. Once said, he could not withdraw it. 'How about your taking up residence here?'

'*Here?*' She stopped buffing the dish. Her face was radiant as she turned it up to him. 'Are you being serious?'

'Yes. Of course. Why not? You know the room. It's dark and not all that comfortable. But, being in the basement, it has it own entrance. And it's own loo and shower.'

'What more could one want? Oh, that's wonderful. Do you really mean it?'

'I wouldn't have suggested it if I didn't.'

'I won't be any trouble.'

'I'm sure you won't.'

'But what rent would you want? Rents here are so high. I wonder if I could afford it.'

'Nothing.'

'Nothing?'

'Nothing.'

He put out a hand and patted her shoulder.

Gradually she brought in possessions of her own, to replace pieces that she carried up to the loft. At first these replacements were from her former flat. Then they were from Portobello Road, or from car boot sales. To these last she began by travelling long distances by public transport. Then, after a few weeks, he urged her to take his car whenever she wished. It was a battered but still beautiful old Daimler, which he himself now rarely used. Sometimes he would accompany her, telling her that something that she fancied was rubbish or advising her to buy this or that chair, table or picture.

One day, he had pointed to a bedside table. 'That's a good piece. Sturdy. Handsome. Victorian.'

She laughed. 'Like you.' She walked round it, examining it. Then she asked the price. 'Oh, gosh!'

'Let me buy it for you.'

'Oh, no! I couldn't agree to that.'

'Of course you could. You've done so many things for me.'

From then on he would often buy objects for her. They always had to be things that he, as well as she, liked.

'You're so good to me.'

'Well, you're so good to me.'

He meant that. She would shop for their meals and cook them, load and empty the dishwasher and the washing machine, iron his shirts, even clean his shoes. Above all, each weekend she worked in the garden. Sometimes that bothered him. It was no longer the garden, overgrown and for the most part shaded, that once he had loved. He found its present order finicky; he hated the sight of once soaring branches now reduced to raw stumps by amputations with an electric saw that she had badgered him into buying. Once it was high summer, it was difficult to find somewhere to sit where the sun did not scorch him.

When he grumbled about that to her, she said: 'Well, you could always get an umbrella.'

'Yes, I could always do that.'

'There's a sale at Habitat. Perhaps they have one. I'll have a look next time I'm passing that way.'

She found the umbrella, he paid for it.

'I feel so old this morning.'

They were sitting at breakfast in the kitchen, she dressed for work and he, as so often, in pyjamas and dressing gown. '*Old?* You certainly don't look it.'

116

'I'm twenty-seven today.'

'*Today*? Why on earth didn't you tell me? We could have had a little party. At all events let me take you out to dinner.'

'Sweet of you. But some friends have arranged something for me. Nothing grand. Just a few people round for drinks and a buffet supper.'

It did not offend him that he had not been invited. He preferred it that she kept her two existences – her one with him, her other of work and friends – in rigorous parallel, never allowing the lines to waver, much less converge.

'I must think what to give you as a present.'

'Oh, no, please! You give me so much already.'

He shook his head. 'I'll think of something.'

Later, sitting out in the only corner of the garden where there was now any shade, he tried to do that. A digital camera? A briefcase to replace her scuffed one? Something for her to wear from Harvey Nicks? Then he decided that, no, he would give her some money. Money was always what people really preferred. Fifty? He stared up into the branches above him. No, no, make it a hundred. Later, he bought a Monet card of water lilies at Givenchy – rather hackneyed, he thought, but never mind – and placed two fifty pounds notes inside it.

When she returned from work, he had the envelope ready. She looked tired, he thought. There were shiny, bruise-like shadows under her eyes, and the eyes themselves were dull.

She opened the envelope. Then she looked up. The eyes suddenly caught fire. 'Oh, you are a darling! How can I thank you?'

'Buy something you want.'

She laughed. 'I wouldn't buy something I *didn't* want.'

'Are you in a hurry for your party?'

'Not really. But I want to have a shower before I change.'

'I have some champagne in the fridge.'

'Oh, I can always find time for champagne.'

After he had poured out the champagne and raised his glass to her, he said: 'A busy day?'

She sighed. 'Yes. And so many people complaining and snapping and being disagreeable. The elderly are the worst.'

'Beware of the elderly!'

'Was that tactless of me? Sorry.'

He shook his head. 'Being old is a battle. So, inevitably, we dinosaurs come out spoiling for a fight.'

There was a silence. She sipped at her glass, then gulped at it. She held it out, tipped it one side as though she were about to empty its contents on to the floor, and then leaned forward. 'May I ask you something?' All at once, she looked taut and pale.

'Of course. Anything.'

'Perhaps I shouldn't. Perhaps it will spoil things.'

'Don't be silly. Go ahead.'

She pondered, licked her lower lip. Then she raised her head and stared at him. 'The thing I want to know...' She stopped, frowning, as though she had forgotten what the thing was.

'Yes? What do you want to know?"

'Well ... Is it true what my mother told me?'

'What did she tell you?'

'That – that you're my father?'

He burst into laughter. 'Oh, did she tell you that?' He shook his head. 'No, I'm afraid it's just not true. I've no idea who was your father but it certainly wasn't me. Yes, of course, we were lovers during most of my time in Bucharest. But I couldn't have been your father. It was physically impossible.'

'You mean you never...?'

'Oh, we went to bed! Often. But...' He shrugged, picked up his glass. 'Well, I just wasn't capable of fathering a child – anyone's child.'

When he had given her the explanation, she put both hands over her mouth and stared at him. Then her whole body was convulsed with a paroxysm of weeping. 'I always believed ... always ... *always*...'

He got up, bent over and put an arm round her heaving shoulders. 'What does it matter? I *think* of you as my daughter. That's what matters. My dream daughter. My adopted daughter.'

The weeping stopped as suddenly as it had begun. She smiled through her tears. She looked up at him. 'Do you mean that? Really mean that?'

'Of course. Of course I do! Your arrival in my life has meant so much to me. Before that, there were often times when I thought that it was pointless to plod on and on. The long, dusty road had begun to have so few pleasures for me. But now...' He laughed. 'But now I'm perfectly happy to continue along it in your company.' He extended a hand to his glass and then raised it. 'To Ana. To my adopted daughter. To our life together. All happiness, dear Ana.'

He raised the glass to his lips.

From then he would often introduce her to guests or to people met by chance when he and she were out to together: 'I don't think you've ever met my adopted daughter Ana, have you?' Some of those people failed to realise that he was being jocular.

She rarely spoke of that other life in which he had no part. He wondered if she spoke to the people in that other life about her life with him. He doubted it. There were occasional references to her colleagues at work – the two women doctors, always so busy and nervy, the one male one, always so lethargic, the practice nurse whose husband had mysteriously killed himself, a fellow receptionist from Uganda, the patients, most of whom she found tiresome in one way or another. There was a cousin, who lived with her partner and a large brood of children – he could never work out how many – in a house out in Teddington. And then there was Henry. 'My friend' – that was how she usually referred to him. 'Tonight I'll be out with my friend.' 'My friend wants me to go to a disco with him.' 'My friend has lent me the latest Ruth Rendell.'

Just to hear her say 'My friend' irritated him. Why couldn't she just refer to him by his name?

Once he said: 'I'd like to meet your friend some day'.

She shook her head: 'Oh, I don't think you'd have anything in common. What would be the point?'

'As you wish.'

That July there was a heat wave. He entered the basement kitchen to fetch some ice for his first Martini of the evening and there she was in only brassiere and knickers, ironing a flimsy, pale-yellow dress. She had told him that she and 'my friend' were going out to dinner. She was in no way disconcerted at his seeing her so scantily clothed. She smiled up to him: 'Gosh, it's hot today, isn't it? Even this kitchen is hot. Usually it's the one cool room in the house.' She licked a forefinger and briefly touched the base of the iron. He forced himself not to look too closely at her. He jerked at the ice-tray.

'Shall I do that for you?' she asked

119

'Oh, no! I can manage. Thank you.'

When he decided to go to bed at his usual hour of eleven, she still had not returned. He double-locked the front door and put the chain across. She had her key to the basement door. He wondered, with a vague, nagging unease, what she and 'my friend' were doing. He continued to wonder as he lay out, covered only by a sheet, and tried to will himself to sleep. He thought of those nipples, briefly glimpsed but vividly remembered as they pushed up through the brassiere, and of those long, bare, oh so beautiful legs. For the first time he was not merely taking pleasure in her youth and her attractiveness, but also longing, with an urgency oddly not unlike the pressure of his bladder that now so often aroused him from sleep, to possess those two things.

Because of the heat, he had left his bedroom door wide open. But for that and his preternatural alertness that night, he would not, a usually heavy sleeper, have heard the sound of the basement door being opened and a brief titter followed by only four audible words ('Whoops! I nearly tripped') in a voice not hers. *She had brought him back.*

He stared up at the ceiling, the back of his hand to his clammy forehead. Then, with a groan, he raised himself and swung his legs out of the bed. The two Nitrazepam tablets, fetched from his dressing-table drawer, felt oddly cold in his sweating palm. Even with repeated gulps of luke-warm water from the glass by his bedside he had difficulty in swallowing them.

He was sitting in the kitchen, *The Times* open on the table beside him. She dashed in.

'I'm late, late, late! Why didn't you wake me?'

He looked up, smiled. He gave no answer. Then he said: 'You came home at some unearthly hour.'

'Yes, my friend insisted on dinner at a restaurant way out towards Acton, and then the service was unbelievably slow.'

'I heard your friend.'

Standing, she had been pouring out coffee from the hastily snatched coffee pot into a cup. The pouring stopped. 'Heard him?'

'Both of you.' He raised his eyebrows in quizzical interrogation.

'Yes, he came in for a moment or two. He wanted me to lend him that DVD of *Chinatown*.'

'I see.'

He knew that she knew that he did not believe her.

'It was rather a boring evening, I'm afraid. He's not exactly a ball of fire.'

'I'd love to meet him. See what he's like. You know, sometimes I almost feel jealous of him.'

She gave a nervous laugh. 'He's nothing much. Civil servants tend to be boring. But he's kind. And he puts up with all my faults and demands.'

'Ah, well.'

She gulped at the coffee, then set down the cup. The clink of cup on saucer seemed to him abnormally loud. He almost expected one or other or both to shatter in the collision.

'Well – see you this evening. I won't be late!'

Then she had gone.

He picked up his cup, tucked *The Times* under his arm, and padded up the stairs and out into the garden. The sun had reached only a far triangle of it. Good! He settled himself in one of the deck chairs, the cup on the ground beside him and *The Times* across his chest. He shut his eyes. He could sleep now. That was what he most wanted. It must be the lingering effect of the pills. He no longer felt any unease, any suppressed rage, any desire to have it out with her. He even felt happy.

It was another year, another summer.

He was lying out, full length, on one of the two deckchairs in the garden and watched her as she walked towards him with the two glasses of Pimm's, frosted with ice, that she had just made for them in the kitchen. He had taught her how to do it. Amazingly she had never heard of a Pimm's, much less known how to make one, until then.

'Thanks.'

She had stooped over him as she handed him the glass. The flimsy cotton dress, low-cut in front, had fallen away briefly to reveal one of her breasts.

He sipped and stared up at the sky, blue with trails of white cloud scurrying across it.

'What a day! What a summer!'

'Yes, indeed,' he said. 'For me – a bonus.'

Again he sipped. Then he shut his eyes. His hip had ceased to ache, he felt totally relaxed. Oddly magnified he could hear the throbbing song of a bird in the tree above him. He could also hear the regular lisp of falling water.

He opened his eyes and swivelled his head to look at her. 'You were right about the fountain. It's wonderful just to sit here and listen to it.'

'And what about the paving?'

'Yes, you were right about that too. This is now the sort of garden that wins prizes.'

She rested her head against the back of her chair and sighed. She looked up at the house. 'I've come to love this house. A dream house. I can hardly believe something like this exists in the heart of London. So beautiful, so quiet. And yet the High Street is only a few minutes away.'

'Last night I had a thought. I've pondered what should happen to the house when I've gone. I love it too. I was born here, you know. My wife died here. I used to think that it should go to my niece. But she'd only sell it. She and that American financier of hers have that huge house in Hampstead. He could buy a house like this with what he earns in a single year. Anyway, what do they ever do for me? I'm lucky if I see them once a month. So – so...' He paused. 'I want you to have it. A dream house for a dream daughter.'

'*Me*?'

'Well, you *are* my adopted daughter. And I know you'd cherish it – as I want it to go on being cherished.'

She leapt up from her chair and stooped over him. 'Oh, you darling! You darling, you darling! Do you really mean this?'

He nodded his head. 'But I have one condition.'

'Yes?'

'I want you to stay with me till – well, till it's all over.'

'Well, of course! Of course!'

She kissed him on one cheek and then other.

'Of course!' she repeated.

He was to give a lecture on 'Eastern Europe and the EU' to a society at his old Oxford college.

'I wished I didn't have to go. It's an effort. It's a bore.'

'Then don't go. Cancel.'

'Oh, I can't do that. Not now.'

'I could ring up for you. Say that you're ill. How about that? I'm a good liar.'

'No. I must keep my word.

'Are they paying you?'

'No. Just expenses.'

'Well, there you are!'

During the dinner that followed his lecture, he was suddenly assailed by the desire to be once more back at home. With Ana. Why not? He wanted to hear only her quiet voice, instead of this Babel of voices of people asking him what he thought of this, that and the other or putting forth their own strident views. He wanted just to look at her. He wanted to know that she was sleeping only a short distance away from him. He was supposed to be spending the night in the college, but the bus from Gloucester Green would take him to Notting Hill Gate in not much over an hour. He got up from the table as soon as he decently could. He had a dentist's appointment the following morning, he lied. He had come to the conclusion that he would rather go to bed late than get up early. He thought he'd go back now.

As he walked towards the house, he saw, with an upsurge of joy, that, though it was now almost one o'clock, the light showed behind the curtains of her bedroom window. He would be able to exchange a few words with her before he went to sleep. But then the thought came to him like a sudden upsurge of bile at the back of the throat: Perhaps Henry was with her? He put his key in the door and entered. From downstairs, he heard the sound of Liszt's Mephisto Waltz No. 1 blaring overloud from the CD player that he had given her for a recent birthday. Some time before he had told her that he wanted to educate her in classical music. He had even persuaded her to accompany him to concerts at the Wigmore Hall. She would hardly be playing that sort of music if Henry were down there, he thought. He stood for a while listening to what, amplified to this degree, sounded like a demonic battering.

The door to her bedroom, at the bottom of the stairs, was open and, from here at their top, he could see her, standing on a small step-ladder that she had placed against the vast Victorian breakfront wardrobe that had once been his mother's. Ana had often said that it was far too large for the room, making it seem cramped. He had agreed with her. But he was sentimental about it. He did not know where else he could put it and he did not want to get rid of it.

He all but called her name. But instead he remained motionless at the top of the stairs and watched her. She was reaching up. She was either placing or replacing something behind one of the two elaborately carved finials surmounting the wardrobe. He continued to watch her as she clambered down the ladder, folded it and rested against the wall beside her. It was only then that he called out: 'Ana! Are you there?'

'You're back!' she cried out. 'I thought you said—'

'I decided not to stay the night. I saw that you had the light on.'

'Yes, I was listening to this wonderful music.'

'Far too loud!'

'I never heard you come in.'

She turned off the music. She asked him about the lecture and the dinner that followed it, she perched on the edge of her bed and he in the one armchair in the room. At one moment she leaned forward to pick up an open pen on the desk beside her and replaced its cap. She continued to hold the pen as they talked.

He did not ask her what she had been doing with the stepladder. Without knowing why, he did not wish to reveal to her his puzzlement and unease.

When she had gone to work, he went down to the basement.

This was something that he would now often do. Suddenly, as though seized by a raging fever, he would succumb to a restlessness that made him wander aimlessly from one room to another, fling himself down on to a deckchair in the garden and then jump up a few seconds later, venture out to buy something for which there was no immediate demand, or toss about on top of the bed hurriedly made by Ana before her departure. Then he would finally give way to the clamorous need so long resisted. He would creep down the stairs, as though she were still in the house and must not suspect what he was doing, and, with accelerating heart, would enter her room.

Perhaps because, unlike him, she so rarely opened the window, he would then be at once assailed by her smell. He would breathe it in deeply, dizzied by it. After that he would start on what he thought of as a quest, though he could not have defined what was its object. He would pick up her lipstick, open it and stare down at it for seconds on end. He would pull out drawers and inspect their contents, even though he now knew exactly what they would contain. She was in the habit of throwing her dirty clothes on to the floor of either one half or the other of the breakfront wardrobe. With a sudden access of breathlessness he would stoop and forage. Then he would bury his face in the object, greedily inhaling its odour.

When, at last sated, he had climbed back up the stairs, the boiling tide of the fever would begin to ebb. At the same time his blood would seem to be similarly ebbing from his body, leaving him feeling inert and cold. Days would then pass, until yet another attack shook him out of his calm daily routine of reading, listening to music, writing long letters to friends whom he now rarely saw, and obsessively completing a number of different crossword puzzles.

Today, his search was not random but focused. He had carried down the stepladder with him. Now he placed it against the breakfront wardrobe, noticing, as he did so, that just below the finial there was the smudge of a palm-print on the highly polished mahogany. Hers, he thought. Swaying a little – his balance was poor these days – he clambered on to the ladder. One step. Two steps. There was a space behind the finial, grey with dust. In it, there lay what looked like a large ledger. He peered down. On the cover of the ledger she had inscribed in her childish hand 'My Diary!'. It struck him as odd that she had followed the two words with an exclamation mark.

He scooped the ledger up in both hands and, once again precariously swaying, descended the ladder. He perched on the edge of the bed (during his secret visits he had so often stretched himself out on this bed in a mingled anguish and abandonment of longing) and raised the cover tentatively, as though he already sensed what lay beneath it.

Dear Diary ... Those were the first words. He had never supposed that anyone nowadays addressed a diary in that way. *I am beginning you as I begin my new life here in what must be one of the most beautiful small houses in London, perhaps in the whole of England or even in the whole world! And there's this secret garden. Unfortunately it's now in a ghastly state. But I'm already doing something about it. At first MR did not want me to change a single thing but I'm beginning to win him over.* MR? It took him a few seconds to realise that the initials stood for himself.

He turned over a few pages. *Even though he's so ancient, he's really not at all bad looking. Sometimes I even think that I could fancy him! I can see why Mamma fell for him. Or did she? In those days, when things were so bad – who knows?*

He sat there, on and on, unaware of the discomfort of leaning forward on the edge of the bed with the ledger resting on his knees. He turned pages at random, back and forth, reading now a few sentences here, now a few sentences there.

H. was thoroughly fed up this evening. He would hardly talk, hardly eat. Then he exploded. He hated what he called This hole and corner business. But what else is one to do? Tell me, Dear Diary. I tried to explain that we must see this thing through. Now that I know for sure that the house is going to be mine it would be MADNESS to throw it all away. Neither H. nor I will ever earn enough to get on the property ladder, the way things are going. We MUST think of the FUTURE!!!

The night before he had been overwhelmed, almost dizzied and nauseated, by the battering of the Liszt Waltz turned to full volume. Now he felt a similar crescendo of battering within him. He could not believe the deviousness, deceit and betrayal that each page revealed. Often a single sentence was like a violent blow. *He denied that he was my father but can one believe him? … I feel so silly when he does his 'adopted daughter' to people he hardly knows … He spent the whole of dinner trying to explain to me what Romania would have to do to join this European Union thing – oh, boring, boring, boring! … A great battle over the fountain but at last I WON…*

He looked at his watch. Impossible! Could he have sat reading this semi-literate stuff for almost an hour? He got up and, holding the ledger to his chest with one hand, he crossed over to the breakfront wardrobe. He reached for the ladder with the other hand. Giddily he climbed the ladder, grimacing with a sudden jab of pain in his right hip each time that he raised his leg. He dropped the ledger into the hollow behind the finial. Some dust rose up, acrid on his tongue and pricking at his eyes.

In the kitchen he awaited her return. Repeatedly he glanced at his watch. She was late. Before him there was a tumbler of vodka on the rocks. He had refilled it twice. He found comforting the trail of fire that each gulp from it set alight in his oesophagus and stomach. Many years ago, after a cancer scare, he had given up smoking. He longed, oh, how he longed, for a cigarette now.

He thought of what he would say to her. *I'm afraid I've reached a decision. I want you to leave. Just as soon as you can go. I don't mind giving you some money for a room somewhere else. I just don't want you here any longer. No,*

I'm not going to give you any reason. No! I'm sorry but there it is. No, Ana, I'm sorry. I don't want any argument. Go! Just go!

Then, disrupting this silent speech, he heard the scrape of her key in the door.

'Hi!'

He did not answer.

'Are you there? Where are you?'

'In the kitchen.'

She came in, a heavily loaded carrier bag in either hand. Her smile was radiant. He noticed how, after having sat for most of the previous day, a Sunday, out in the sun-drenched garden, her forehead and cheeks were glowing. So were her bare arms. On them he could see, with extraordinary clarity, the fine golden hairs.

'I'm sorry I'm so late. You must be starving. I was looking for some of those spectacle wipe things that you said that you wanted. Boot's in the High Street had sold out, so I took the 328 down to Earls Court. I also got you some of those violet and rose creams.' She was now taking her purchases out of the two bags and placing them on the kitchen table beside his tumbler of vodka. 'I'll get things ready in a jiffy. What a wonderful invention the microwave is!'

Suddenly he found that he could expel not one of that swarm of words that had been angrily buzzing in his brain ever since he had left her room.

He thought: *I need her.*

He thought: *How am I ever to manage without her?*

He thought: *I must keep her to see me out.*

'What sort of day did you have?'

'Not bad. Nothing all that interesting. For me one day is now very much like another.'

He had never cared for this young man with his small, myopic eyes behind huge horn-rimmed glasses and his large nose and ears. Odd that his father, who had had so much charm, had produced an only child with so little of it. But charm was not what one required from a solicitor. What one required was efficiency, honesty and discretion.

'This time I've made it easy. I'm doing away with all those different legacies. With the exception of a few small sums, I want everything –

127

everything – to go to my old Oxford college. They can do with it what they like. No stipulations. If they want to use it for some nonsense or other, then good luck to them. I just don't care.'

The college was the richest in Oxford. That they did not need the money had been his chief incentive in leaving it to them.

'I've put a lot of things in the freezer. You only have to heat them up in the microwave.'

Ana and 'my friend' were leaving for a long weekend in France, spent in exploring World War I battlefields. 'He's got a thing about them,' she had explained. 'Don't ask me why. I know that I'm going to be horribly bored. But he so often does things that I want to do but he doesn't, that I feel that I must make the same sacrifice for him once in a while.'

'Thank you. You shouldn't have gone to all that trouble.'

'Are you sure you'll be all right?'

'Oh, yes. Thank you. Fine.'

'I really don't like leaving you.' She lowered her head and put her lips to his cheek. 'Just ring me if you need me. You have my number?'

'Oh, yes, I have your number.'

As she turned away, he felt exhilarated that she had failed to notice the sardonic double entendre. The lines came back to him: *The sunlight on the garden hardens and grows cold.* He felt the hardness and coldness within him with a soaring sense of triumph.

Now You See It

In the late afternoon, Tony dawdled along the Corniche. He had thought that this winter visit to Luxor – of which he had made others in the past, not alone but always with Mark – would thaw out the block of ice, a combination of grief, guilt and a hopeless resignation, in which for weeks now he had felt himself to be rigidly embedded. He had invited a number of friends, both male and female, to come with him, but they had all made their often flimsy excuses. Unhappiness can carry a contagion and they were wary of it.

A tall, muscular boy, sixteen or seventeen at a guess, with large hands, a large nose and a tousled mop of hair, loomed up in his path. He was wearing a tattered, stained djellabah that all but covered his trainers. 'Hello!' he greeted Tony.

Tony stared at him, his eyes dull. Then he muttered 'Hello' and began to move on.

'Where you from?' The boy was at his heels.

'Where am I from? From England. Have you ever visited England?' He at once regretted the question. It would make it more difficult to get rid of the boy, and in any case it was a ludicrous one. Was it likely that such a boy had ever travelled even to Cairo?

'No visit. Never.' The boy pointed at his chest. 'Poor. Want visit England. But – poor, poor. No money. How many day Luxor?'

'Well, I arrived only yesterday.'

131

Tony was reluctant to say more. He had replied only out of the habit
of politeness.

'You go West Bank?'

Tony slapped out at a fly that kept hovering around him. He might
have been slapping out at the boy. 'Yes, I was there this morning. And I
plan to go there again tomorrow.'The block of ice shifted inside him.The
sun suddenly felt warm on his bare arms and forehead.

'You want taxi?'

'No. Thank you. I usually get one outside the hotel...'

'I have cousin. Good taxi. Very cheap. Hotel taxi, much money. I
arrange taxi tomorrow. I come with you. Guide. Yes? My name Abdul.
Abdul. Everyone know Abdul.'

'Well ... Well, that's very kind of you. But...'Then, on a crazy impulse,
he nodded: 'Oh, all right.Yes. Why not?'

'Well, where's this taxi?'

Tony had been obliged to take two Imodium tablets that morning, and
the back pocket of his trousers was stuffed with lavatory paper. He had all
but decided to spend the day at the hotel.

Abdul pointed up the steep, uneven path that led from the crowded
West Bank quay into the village above it.

'But all the taxis are here.'

'Cousin wait in cool place. Not far. Taxi cool.'

Tony's stomach was again churning, and he had suddenly become
aware that his new shoes were pinching feet swollen in the heat. Should
he swallow one more of the tablets that he was carrying in the breast
pocket of his jacket? This was ridiculous.The taxi might be cool, but he
was getting extremely hot trudging up the path.

There was a long silence except for Tony's increasingly laboured
breathing. Then: 'There is taxi!' Abdul cried. But what he was pointing at
was a pristine minibus, with 'Cleopatra Tours' emblazoned on its side.

'That's not a taxi.'

'Yes, yes, cousin's taxi.'

The driver, a middle-aged man with a straggly moustache and a face
pitted with either acne or smallpox, put aside the newspaper that he had
been reading and descended stiffly from the driving-seat. Unlike Abdul's
brown, stained djellabah, his was white and spotless. 'Hello!' he greeted

Tony. 'Me Mohammed.' He grinned. One of his front teeth was missing.

Tony merely nodded. Then he turned to Abdul. 'We'd better first fix a price.' He turned back to the driver. 'How much?'

'One hundred fifty. Egyptian pound. Cheap. Special price. You friend Abdul. Abdul my cousin.'

Tony began to argue. Ridiculous! On his Luxor visit the previous year he had paid a mere fifty Egyptian pounds for a taxi for a whole day. But his heart was not in it. Soon, a sum of sixty was reached. Tony would often tell people that he hated any disagreement, argument or row. Such things made him feel ill, he would say.

'Well, that's settled.' Having clambered into the mini-bus, Tony briefly patted Abdul's knee with a sigh. 'Now we can enjoy a lovely day.' He was amazed when Abdul took his hand in his and with the other hand began to stroke it. There was something exciting both in the spontaneity of the move and in the abrasive contact of that callused palm.

By now Tony had decided that he had worked out for himself the truth about the 'taxi'. Cleopatra Travel must employ Mohammed as a driver, ferrying customers from and to the airport and around the town. This was his day off. He had 'borrowed' the mini-bus to make some extra money. Of that extra money, Abdul would no doubt get his cut.

The flank of a mountain embraced the whole site of the Hatshepsut temple like the wings of some vast, hovering solar disc. The three terraces, stacked one above the other, radiated an almost unbearable heat and dazzle.

All at once, Tony felt a terrible thirst. Perhaps it was all the sweating he thought. Or perhaps the effect of the over-salted, tough lamb bacon that he had speared from the buffet at breakfast to accompany some dry, floury scrambled egg.

He paused in his ascent, a hand pressed into the small of his back.

'Thirsty.'

'You thirsty?'

Tony nodded.

'I get water. Wait!'

'No, it doesn't matter.'

But Abdul had already begun to race down the incline towards a row of kiosks. He was not a bad boy, Tony thought. Willing. And really quite handsome. With a sigh he continued his laborious ascent up the ramp.

133

Then, just as he was about to reach the first of the three terraces, he felt a slithering in his gut, as though some reptile were lazily moving there, followed by a sharp tweak of pain. Christ! He began to hurry back down the ramp. At the bottom, surrounded by jabbering, sweating tourists, he looked frantically around him. No lavatory in sight. No Abdul in sight. Desperate, he lurched off into the blazing heat, across a bare landscape littered with stones and fragments of masonry. Eventually he came on an empty hut, tilted sideways, its door ajar and its wooden floor rotten. He squatted behind it. If anyone saw him, too bad!

Just as he had lowered himself into position, his immaculate trousers trailing in the dust round his ankles, he heard a scrabbling sound. Oh, hell!

But instead of the expected tourist or labourer, it was a long-eared, jackal-like dog, its coat a dusty grey. Having sloped round the hut, it seated itself four or five yards in front of him. It stared at him. Then it closed its slanting, mica-black eyes, raised its head and slowly opened its mouth, revealing small, needle-sharp teeth. Tony thought that it was going to emit a howl, but instead it merely yawned. Once again it fixed its eyes on him. He had seen a head exactly like that in the museum the previous afternoon. It belonged to a statue of the god Anubis, who escorted the souls of the dead into the presence of the judge of the infernal regions. He and the dog stared at each other for several seconds. Then Tony felt passing through him the emotional equivalent of the reptilian gliding through the gut that had brought him to this spot. In panic he defecated in an explosive burst. Half standing, half crouching, he scrabbled in the back pocket of his trousers for some tissues.

As he returned up the ramp to the temple, the dog pattered behind him. But, on their approach to its entrance, it suddenly shot off at an angle, to make for Abdul, who was standing at the far end of the terrace, a bottle of mineral water under an arm as he stared downwards, clearly in search of Tony. The dog jumped up, its paws on Abdul's knees, making the boy rear away in terror. Then he kicked out viciously. The dog let out a shrill squeal, bared its teeth and, tail between legs, scampered off, zigzag, into the crowd. Tony felt a queasy horror.

Abdul waved the bottle in greeting. It was as though, in a few seconds, he had already forgotten of the incident with the dog. 'Where you go? I look everywhere.' He held out the bottle. 'Cold.'

Gratefully Tony took the bottle, unscrewed its cap and sipped and then gulped. 'What do I owe you?' The boy looked puzzled. 'How much?'

'Nothing, nothing. Present.' He waved his hand back and forth in front of his face, as though to fan it.

'Well, that's very kind of you.' Tony was grudging. Cynically he had decided that this act of generosity was merely a bait for a larger tip than he might otherwise have given at the end of the day.

With what struck Tony as glee, Abdul now began to speak of the terrorist massacre that had taken place on this spot only two years before. 'Many, many killed. There – there!' He pointed. 'Much blood.' He gave a staccato laugh, which seemed to erupt from the back of his throat.

'Where's Mohammed?' Tony demanded. He wanted to get away. 'This place gives me the creeps.'

'Creeps?'

'It stinks of death. Haunted by all those wretched murdered people.'

Abdul laughed. He clearly had not understood. He pointed. 'More blood over there. There! *There!* Look, look! Blood!'

That night, Tony thought of Mark. Mark had died of leukaemia, but all their friends had decided that he must really have died of Aids. How typical of Tony, they had said among themselves, that he should refuse to own up to the truth. The fact was, they said, that he had always been ashamed that he was gay. That was because of his upbringing, of course – his mother a vicar's daughter, his father an army colonel, or was it a general?

Tony thought of Mark with a guilt that gnawed at him like the pain that all day had gnawed at his bowels until at long last, late in the evening, the Imodium had had some effect. Against all expectation and against his will, he had been attracted to Abdul. Coming home in the late, cooling dusk, he had moved closer to him in the mini-bus, hoping that Mohammed in front would not notice. Now it was he who had taken Abdul's hand in his, instead of the other way around. His fingers had moved slowly and gently over the callused right palm, as though tracing the lines on it.

Oh, Mark, forgive me, forgive me!

Soon Tony wanted to spend every hour of every day with Abdul.

On their second evening together, Abdul insisted on taking him to a restaurant above a spice shop in the souk. The food, piled high on each plate, had been so disgusting that Tony had left most of it. When he had eventually managed to get the bill, it was ludicrously expensive and he had ended up, uncharacteristically and much to Abdul's dismay, shouting first at the waiter, who knew no English, and then at the proprietor, who had shuffled out from a curtained recess, puffing at a long, malodorous cheroot, to see what the row was all about. Eventually, having realised that he had met his match, the proprietor had murmured 'Okay, okay. For my friends I take away twenty,' and had amended the bill. Tony's only response had been 'What barefaced cheek!' – which neither the proprietor nor Abdul had understood, both of them now smiling in relief and gratitude at him.

Tony knew that he was being constantly cheated into paying over the odds. But, if the sums were so small, what did it matter? If one was as poor as Abdul – his father dead, a number of younger brothers and sisters dependent on him, as he had more than once related – it was understandable that, having met a foreigner, he should take him for all he could. To such people all tourists, other than the most youthful, must seem to be millionaires. After all, the Hilton was charging for a night far more than Abdul would ever earn in a month.

A small boy in an overlarge djellabah carried out most of the work of sailing the felucca, at the barked instructions of the stout, taciturn captain, another of Abdul's 'cousins'. Unlike most Egyptians, the captain made no attempt to ingratiate himself with his foreign customer. He grunted as he put out a hand to help Tony aboard. He pointed to where he and Abdul should sit on some cushions. Then he turned away, to squat as far away from them as possible.

As the felucca lazily tacked back and forth from one side of the river to the other, Abdul and Tony, perched side by side, held each other's hands. They talked little but from time to time one or the other would turn his head and they would smile simultaneously.

Once in midstream, the captain began to roll himself a joint. Having puffed at it for a while, eyes half-closed, he slowly got up, waddled over to Abdul and handed it to him. Abdul drew on it three or four times, gave a dreamy smile, and then extended the pinched remains of it to Tony.

Tony drew back. 'Oh, no. No, thank you. I don't smoke.' From the smell, he knew what he was being offered.

'Good', Abdul said, once again holding out the joint. He gave that joyous laugh of his that always had the effect of filling Tony with an answering joy. 'Good,' he said. 'Make happy.'

Tony wanted to say 'But I'm happy – wonderfully happy – already.' But to please Abdul he took the joint and cautiously drew on it. Then he held it out. 'Thank you.'

'More, more!' Abdul urged, laughing.

Tony shook his head.

Leaving the captain and the boy on the felucca, Tony and Abdul wandered through the banana plantation on the island that had been their destination. Recklessly, even though they kept meeting other tourists, Tony would from time to time succumb to the perilous craving to embrace Abdul, his mouth glued to his. Abdul resisted at first, then showed an equal ardour. Tony could feel the boy's cock hard against him, through the thick, stained fabric of the djellabah. On one occasion three Japanese women came on them in one of these embraces. One put a hand up to her mouth and giggled behind it, one let out a brief squawk, and the third stared, round-eyed. Briefly they halted. Then, like startled deer, they swerved off on to another path. Eventually, Abdul caught Tony by the hand and attempted to drag him down an incline towards a rubbish tip. But Tony, remembering the recent case of a group of Cairo men savagely sentenced to four or five years in prison merely for having attended a gay party, pulled away and shook his head.

As they boarded the felucca, he thought what a coward he had been to reject that opportunity. But then, as first the sky and then the waters began to darken, and he sat beside Abdul, an arm round his shoulders and their bodies so close that the two of them seemed to have been melded into one, he had no regrets. I have never been so happy, he thought, Mark totally forgotten. Never. He removed his hand from Abdul's shoulder and ran the fingers of it through the boy's dry, dusty hair. Abdul laughed and brushed his own hand slowly down Tony's cheek.

Soon after that, the felucca was in trouble. Having hugged the west bank of the river for a considerable time, it all but tipped over at a capricious gust of a wind and grated to a standstill. The captain shouted angrily at his diminutive assistant, who, still in his djellabah, at once jumped into the opaque water and began to tug on a rope thrown down to him. The captain then struggled with a metal shaft protruding from the middle of the boat – to raise the rudder, Tony assumed. Abdul joined him.

The two men tugged in turn. At last the boat began to move. Abdul laughed and held up his hand. Somehow he had managed to nick his middle finger on the metal shaft. Blood trickled from it.

'Oh, look what you've done!' Tony cried out in dismay. He felt in the back pocket of his shorts and produced some tissues. 'Here.'

'Nothing, nothing.'

'Don't be silly. Come here!'

Abdul went across. He held out his hand.

Tony surprised himself by what he did next. Instead of wrapping the finger in the tissues, he raised it to his mouth. He sucked on it.

The blood tasted strangely metallic and bitter. He had never tasted blood like that before. Greedily he sucked on it again. It filled him with a dizzying rapture.

Tony knew that the calèche driver was making a huge detour on the way from the restaurant owned by another of Abdul's 'cousins' back to the hotel. But so far from objecting, he was glad of it. Heavenly, heavenly, to sit like this, so close to Abdul, his hand on his cock and Abdul's hand on his, with the immense sky, pricked by innumerable stars, above them, and the emaciated horse, from time to time galvanised into a stumbling trot by a lash of the whip, clip-clopping up one narrow, dark, deserted street after another.

There was a removable metal barrier across the entrance to the hotel drive. A soldier was seated on a stool beside it, a rifle across his knees. No calèche, the driver indicated, was allowed to proceed any further. Abdul jumped out and then held out a hand to help Tony down. The driver named a sum and, though he knew it to be exorbitant, Tony paid at once, not grudgingly but with a curious sense of euphoric liberation.

As the calèche creaked round in a half-circle, Tony suddenly thought of how Abdul would get home. 'Stop! Stop!' he called out. But the driver either did not hear or decided to ignore the summons for fear that Tony was going to demand back some of the overpayment.

'We must find a taxi for you.'

'No, no! Not necessary! I walk to bus.'

'But will there be a bus at this hour?'

'Maybe.' Abdul did not seem at all worried.

'Oh, I wish I could take you into the hotel.' Tony said it with an extraordinary intensity of longing. They had spoken about this before. But

Abdul had said that it was out of the question, and Tony had known that he was right. Since the events of September 11, two armed policemen frisked anyone, even a tourist, who wished to enter the hotel. With Tony these two men had always been flirtatious. But they would not be flirtatious with Abdul, quite the reverse. There were also at least half-a-dozen men on guard in the grounds.

'Oh, I so much want to hold you in my arms in my bedroom – to show you how much I love you … Why, why, why do things have to be so difficult?'

'I find a way.' Abdul nodded gravely, then repeated: 'I find a way.'

'But how? How?'

The soldier had turned his head and was staring at them. But, as in the banana plantation, Tony, usually so cautious and conventional, did not care. He took Abdul in his arms and kissed him on the mouth. 'Goodnight, my darling.' Once again he could feel that cock hard against him through the djellabah. He must have been wrong. The boy must, must, must have some feelings for him. It was not just a question of money. 'We'll have to say goodbye here.'

Again they embraced. Again Tony felt that cock hard against him.

As, alone now, Tony approached the hotel, he saw a greyish shadow imposed on the hunched shape of a bush to the left of the entrance. Oddly, the shadow seemed to flicker as though it were a paper cut-out in a wind. He halted, peered. He had at first thought that it must be one of the feral cats that, voracious but wary, stalked the area round the poolside restaurant, waiting for someone to chuck over to them a scrap of gristle, a prawn-shell or a fish head. But now he realised that it was a dog. All at once he remembered that jackal-like Anubis dog with the long, pricked ears and slanting eyes, at which Abdul, in a panic, had kicked out. This dog exactly resembled that one. But it couldn't be the same dog. How could it have crossed the river? The breed must be a common Egyptian one. He was about to push at the swing-door into the hotel, then turned and looked round again. *Now you see it, now you don't.* He heard a faint click, as of a camera shutter. With that click, the dog had vanished…

Oh, no doubt, it had slunk back out of sight into the bush. But as the lift carried him the four floors up to his room, he felt a lingering unease.

Yes, there had been a definite click and simultaneously an invisible hand had erased that tremulous, grey shadow. Weird.

Tony, who so often boasted that he fell asleep as soon as his head had touched the pillow, now could not sleep. He lay with his hands crossed behind his head on the vast double bed and stared up at the ceiling. He had forgotten the disquieting mystery of the dog. He still felt sexually aroused. He wondered whether to toss himself off. On his rare nights of insomnia, he had always found that that was the most effective sleeping pill of all. He began to imagine to himself Abdul's journey home – the waiting for a long deferred and overcrowded bus, the ill-lit, dilapidated ferry nudging its clumsy way across the river, the walk up the steep path to the mud-house, its windows unglazed apertures, that Abdul had pointed out to him...

He was startled from his reverie by a tap-tapping sound. Was it coming from the next-door room, occupied by a young American couple with whom, from time to time, he exchanged a few words? He raised himself on an elbow, his senses alert. He was uncomfortably aware of the hastening beat of his heart. The tap-tapping was coming from the balcony.

He clambered out of bed, hesitated, then crossed over to the window. Cautiously, he pulled back the heavy curtain and peered out, a hand raised to his eyes.

It was Abdul. He was smiling, the tip of his tongue showing between teeth startlingly white in the moonlight. Tony hurried to unbolt the door and then to open the wire screen beyond it. Without saying a word, Abdul slipped into the room and closed the screen and door behind him. He was sweating from the exertion of having reached the balcony.

'How did you get up here?'

In his halting English, gesticulating and laughing excitedly between sentences and even phrases, Abdul explained. Workmen were renovating one wing of the hotel. There was scaffolding. Hadn't Tony noticed? He had crossed a field, that field overlooked by the balcony, scaled a low wall, and then climbed up the scaffolding. He had worked his way along the roof of the wing and jumped from that roof on to the one just above the fourth storey. From there he had lowered himself down on to the balcony. It was lucky that the previous evening, as they had walked along the path between the river and the gardens of the hotel, Tony had pointed out his balcony, the last on the fourth floor on that side of the hotel.

'But you shouldn't have taken such a risk! Crazy, crazy!' But secretly Abdul's courage and enterprise thrilled Tony.

First Abdul had to inspect everything. He opened drawers, examined the various toiletries in the bathroom and even took off the stopper of a small flask of shampoo to sniff at it, flushed the lavatory, turned the air-conditioning up and down, switched the various lights off and on, and bounced on the bed. Then he pulled the dusty, tattered djellabah off over his head and, seated naked on a chair, removed his trainers. Tony went up behind him, stooped and put his arms around him. But first Abdul insisted on having a shower. For a time, Tony watched as the water cascaded over the muscular body. Then, on a sudden impulse, he hurriedly pulled off his pyjamas and himself stepped into the shower. He held Abdul close, his face against his shoulder. He gasped for breath as the water splashed on to the pair of them. They both began to laugh more and more loudly until Tony, mindful of the American couple, put a hand over Abdul's mouth. 'Sh!'

Later, after they had made love, Tony scrambled off the bed and looked down at Abdul's still naked body. 'Oh, if only I had a photograph of you! If only I had a camera! My friend Mark was always the photographer on our expeditions.'

'You want photograph?'

'Oh, yes, yes! So that when I'm back in England, I can look at you.'

'I bring photograph. Tomorrow. French friend take photograph. I bring.'

Tony felt a wasp sting of jealousy. 'French friend? What friend? Do you mean lover?'

Abdul laughed. 'Not what you think! Married. Travel on cousin's felucca, wife, children, two children.'

Tony did not believe him. But he no longer cared.

When the dawn was about to break, Abdul said that he must go. Otherwise the police might see him. Hurriedly he dressed. Then, careful to make no sound, he opened first the door to the balcony and next the wire screen. Tony held out the handful of ten-dollar notes that he had fetched from his room safe while Abdul had been dressing.

'No, no!'

'Yes. Please! I want you to have this.'

Without any further hesitation Abdul took the money and tucked it into a pocket inside the voluminous djellabah. 'See you again.'

'See you tomorrow. Same place. Eleven.'

They kissed. Then kissed again and yet again.

'Don't forget the photograph.'

'Photograph – yes, remember, remember!'

'Promise!'

'Promise. Abdul always keep promise.'

Tony craned his head to watch as, with extraordinary agility, Abdul swung himself up from the balcony and on to the roof. For a moment the boy stood there, outlined against a sky now streaked with the pale yellow of the dawn just breaking. The air was chill. He waved, smiled, waved. Then he was gone.

Tony remained on the balcony in only his pyjama trousers. He clutched its rail, looked down. Suddenly, a grey streak seared his eyeballs, moving at extraordinary speed across the dim garden below. He thought: the dog!

Then he heard the shot. It was followed by three more.

'I should have gone down,' Tony later told an elderly, military-looking gay man, also on holiday alone at the hotel, when they had struck up a conversation by the pool.

'What would have been the point? He was dead. You would have been implicated. They might have arrested you. They'd have certainly questioned you. You might have missed the plane back to England.'

'I should have gone down. It was a kind of betrayal.'

'Don't be silly. … But what a crazy thing for him to do. Guards everywhere. Armed. Nervous. Trigger-happy. Crazy.'

'It was my fault. My fault. I'll never forgive myself.'

After dinner, while the elderly man sat in the library rereading one of his guidebooks, Tony restlessly wandered the garden. He half hoped and half feared that he would once again see the jackal-like dog. But there was no sign of it. Three policemen sat round the pool, each with a gun across his knees. They were talking in low voices, punctuated by boisterous laughter. Perhaps it was one of them who had killed Abdul.

Tony decided to go up to his room. As he entered the lift, his two American neighbours staggered into it after him. This was not the first time when he had seen them drunk after dinner. They greeted him cheerfully and the man said: 'Having fun?'

Tony merely shrugged.

As the three of them walked down the corridor, the American woman said: 'You remember those shots last night? Apparently it was someone trying to break into the hotel. That receptionist – the one with the squint – just told us. We're not supposed to know, of course. The authorities are trying to hush it up. Might put off tourists.'

'It makes one nervous,' the man took up. 'He could have been a terrorist. He could have blown us all to hell.'

As he put his key in the door, Tony heard the sound of splashing. Had he left the shower on? Hurriedly he opened the bathroom door. The light was on, the floor was awash, as it had been on that night when he and Abdul had stood clutching each other under the battering of the water. But the shower was now off.

Puzzled and in growing apprehension, he left the bathroom and went into the bedroom. The window to the balcony and the wire screen were open. Then he realised that there was something on his pillow. He went over and stooped to pick it up. It was a snapshot of Abdul standing nude by open French windows, with the out-of-focus blur of a tree beyond him. Under the tree there was an amorphous grey shape. Was it – could it be – that jackal-like dog crouching there? Tony stared down at the photograph for a long time. He could not be sure.

Then he became aware of a stickiness on his forefinger and middle finger, and at the same time saw that something had been written across the bottom of the snapshot in Arabic.

He examined his fingers with a mixture of amazement and mounting terror. They were sticky with blood. He put the fingers to his mouth and sucked them. The blood tasted strangely metallic and bitter. He felt that he was about to retch. It might have been a poison.

Of course the elderly man had his brusque, matter-of-fact explanation. He was a man who always did.

For some reason – probably the sort of blockage that constantly occurred with Egyptian plumbing – the water from the shower that Tony had taken before dinner had been regurgitated up the waste pipe. Or perhaps one of the floor staff had decided to take a shower while Tony was at dinner.

And the photograph? Well, it was not impossible that that same member of the floor staff had been a friend or even a relative of Abdul and so, having known of the affair, had decided to leave that image of the dead man on Tony's pillow. Why not? It was just the sort of sentimental gesture one might expect from an Egyptian.

And the blood? Oh, it could be that the person who had left the photograph had not, after all, been a member of the staff. Perhaps, instead, it was the 'cousin' who had driven them in the mini-bus. In that case, he might have climbed into the room as Abdul had climbed into it and had then somehow cut his hand while doing so. Wasn't that a possibility?

But obstinately Tony kept shaking his head. 'No, no,' he said. Then loudly and decisively: 'No!'

Back in Brighton, Tony showed the photograph to the Algerian lover of a friend of his. Could he translate the inscription?

The Algerian peered down, then looked up. 'Oum Khaltoum,' he said. He went on to explain that the words were from a song made popular by the most famous of Arab singers of her time.

'What do they say?'

The Algerian pursed his lips and frowned. Then he ventured: 'Death conquers life. But love conquers death.'

Tony gave a little gasp and raised a hand to his eyes, as though to shield them from a sudden glare.

The Algerian again peered down at the photograph. 'There's something else here. The writing is bad. An uneducated man must have written it. Yes.' He himself was an educated man, a radiologist. He peered again. 'With my love. Forever. And signed,' he added. 'Signed "Abdul".' He looked up, laughed. 'Who is this Abdul? A boy-friend?'

At first Tony kept the photograph on his bedside table, in a frame specially bought for it. Then, when he looked at it — which he did less and less — he noticed that it was beginning to fade. The sun must be causing that, he decided, and placed the photograph in a Florentine tooled leather box in which he kept such things as studs, cuff links, collar-stiffeners and safety pins. On the rare occasions that he had recourse to the box he realised with a mingling of dismay and bewilderment that the fading was continuing.

Seven months later, having just returned from what he was later to describe as an 'utterly blissful' holiday in Thailand, Tony was dressing to go to Glyndebourne with a party of friends. He opened the Florentine leather box to get out a pair of cuff links and studs for the old-fashioned dress shirt that he now so rarely wore. To his amazement he then found that the surface of the snapshot had become little more than a blank, milky expanse. How could that have happened? As with the dog on that horrible night in Luxor: *Now you see it, now you don't.*

Oh, probably the man who had printed the snapshot had used some primitive process, he hastily told himself, that resulted in rapid fading.

But then – the thought suddenly came to him – why had both the bloodstain and Abdul's scrawl also vanished?

His lips trembled. The hands holding the snapshot began to shake uncontrollably. He rarely now thought of Abdul. When he did so, it was without any of the old anguish of recollection and frustrated longing. Abdul was now one with Mark. Nothing lasted. Nothing. That was the hellish thing about life. And love.

With a single convulsive movement he tore the snapshot into two and then, in mounting frenzy, into innumerable tiny scraps.

Dreams

It is the break and ache of day. Yesterday I awoke to those words. They were a fragment of some monument that all through the night I had been struggling to build. The words were no longer only in my mind but now also on my lips. I whispered them. *It is the break and ache of day.* But of the complex construct of which all through my sleeping hours they had been merely a tiny part, I now remembered nothing.

It is in words, not images, that I now almost invariably dream. All my life I have been, above all, a wordsmith. When so many other, less important, of my attributes have vanished or are vanishing, that still remains. In consequence, I am becoming more and more like that old man, a famous jeweller, who was my neighbour in Japan some forty years ago. He could not remember his wife's or children's names or, often, even his own. He could not remember how to knot a tie or fasten his shoe-laces or pour a glass of iced tea or find his way to the primitive privy in a wooden shed at the bottom of his narrow, overgrown garden. But each day he sat at his work-bench in a contented abstraction not merely from the world but also from an eighty-three years accumulation of memories, now inaccessible to him, while he still fashioned, with all his old consummate artistry, some brooch, bracelet or necklace. Fascinated and admiring, I used to watch him. Occasionally, he would look up and across at me and give me a vague, happy smile.

But this morning it was different. I had dreamed not in words but in images. One of those images remained with me, so vivid that I still saw it

149

in every minute detail even as I felt the battering of the alarm clock and opened my eyes. The image is of a wave-like curve of balcony, constructed of wooden slats, many of which have rotted. It overlooks a cliff-like incline, so that the tops of trees all but brush one's feet as one looks over it. Its railings are a greenish blue, the paint cracked and peeling. Behind it is the low annexe to the farmhouse, with its identical rooms each with its French windows. The paying guests in the annexe usually keep their curtains drawn even in daytime, since otherwise anyone on the balcony can glance in on them.

With an effort, I banish the image, so seductive and yet potentially so dangerous. Then I fall, rather than clamber, out of bed and, hand to banister to steady myself, creak down to the kitchen to make my wife's morning tea. Some months ago she moved to the bedroom on the floor below mine to avoid being kept awake by my muttering in my sleep of those innumerable words that all through the night jostle for attention in a fatigued, failing brain craving only for the respite of silence. 'How did you sleep?' She stares up at me, as though a stranger were asking some obtrusive question. 'Oh, you know how it is.' Yes, I know how it is, having so often heard how it is. The restless legs. The nag of pain in the back. The mosquito whine of tinnitus in her left ear.

Instead of at once shaving and taking my bath, I return to my bedroom and lie out on the bed. I do not bother to pull the bedclothes over me. I am unaware of the cold. I close my eyes. I entreat the banished memory of my balcony dream to come back to me...

On that balcony a boy of thirteen is sitting on a folding canvas chair. It is afternoon. He can hear, in the distance, his mother tinkling at the upright Pleyel piano in the Ardennes farmhouse. She often complains, even to the Belgian farmer and his wife, that the piano is out of tune. They look bewildered, as though they did not understand her, even though she has spoken in perfectly correct French, albeit with a heavy English accent. Then one or other of them shrugs, smiles and says something like '*Eh bien, madame* ...' They will do nothing about the piano, just as they will do nothing about the dripping tap of her wash-basin or the curtain that, missing a ring, lets in a narrow wedge of light to prod her awake far too early every summer morning of that holiday. The boy's older brother is out, gun at the ready, with the bearded, taciturn farmer. They will usually return each with at least a brace of rabbits. The boy hates the rabbit casserole that everyone else finds so delicious. He eats a mouthful or two, then pushes it to one side – 'I'm not really hungry' he tells his mother in a fretful voice when she enquires why he isn't eating.

Now, on the balcony, he is halfway through the *Collected Works* of Tennyson, in a leather-bound copy that belonged to his recently dead father. If his father were still alive, they would be staying in some elegant hotel and not in this farmhouse, recommended to them as 'amazing value' by one of his mother's bridge-playing friends. Already he recognises in Tennyson someone who is obsessed with words – their appearance on the page, their subtle gradations of meaning, above all their initial sounds and then the other sounds that resonate on and on from them – even as he himself is already obsessed with words. His brother, seventeen years old and about to become a Sandhurst cadet and eventually to be killed on a Normandy beach, laughs at this passion for Tennyson. He puts on a voice, melodramatic and comically cockney, as he intones: '*Come into the garden, Maud.*' There is something ludicrous about the name Maud, even the boy can see that.

The afternoon sun is in his eyes. He hears a far-off shot. He winces as he imagines the rabbit leaping into the air and then crashing down on the hard surface of a field baked dry by day after day of furnace heat. A voice speaks behind him. It is deep and resonant, the accent German. The boy has not heard any approach, since the man is wearing plimsolls. 'What are you reading?'

The boy swivels his head. He has already seen this squat, muscular man, with the flat, oddly expressionless face and large sunburned hands, the nails savagely bitten, at breakfast that morning. Having entered the long, narrow room, the man then bowed and intoned with an almost comic gravity: '*Bonjour, messieurs, bonjour, mesdames.*' Much later, his wife, thin and anxious-looking in a pale-blue cotton dress, her face heavily powdered, slipped through the door. She gave no spoken greeting to the assembled company, merely a bow smaller and far more hesitant than her husband's. He extended a hand to her. She took it with a look of beseeching gratitude. Suddenly the anxious-looking face was irradiated by joy. Later the boy's mother learned from the farmer's wife that the couple were on their honeymoon. They came from Düsseldorf, the farmer's wife said, and both of them were teachers.

The man stoops over the boy. He looks down at the book. 'Poetry?' The man must have realised that from the way that the lines are laid out on the page. The boy nods. 'Who is the poet?' There is an odd formality in the way in which the words emerge from under the man's closely clipped moustache.

'Tennyson,' the boy replies. There is a quaver in his voice. He might be attempting an answer to a difficult question back at school. He feels a mounting excitement, as though a swarm of bees were buzzing inside him. 'D'you know his work?'

The man shakes his head. ' Sorry. Heine. You know Heine?'

'Not really. No.'

'He is good. Very good. Genius. You must read.'

'I don't know any German.'

'In English. I am sure there is translation.'

The man is bending even lower over the chair. Suddenly the boy is aware of the hand in the man's trouser pocket. He cannot help noticing it, it is so near to his elbow. As though he has realised that the boy has noticed that hand and what the hand is attempting to restrain, the man walks stiffly over to a distant chair and then returns with it. He places it beside the boy's and sits down, crossing one leg high over the other. They begin to talk.

The man asks about the boy and his family. The boy speaks about his father, brilliant, reserved and never ill before his sudden, premature death from a heart-attack, and about his mother, who is half-American and who was briefly on the stage. The man talks about his life as a schoolmaster and his passion for sports. He teaches gymnastics, he explains. He had hoped to be chosen for the German gymnastic team for the 1936 Olympic Games but – he shrugs, his shoulders droop – at the last moment...

'I'm no good at sports. Hopeless. My brother's in the Rugby fifteen at our school. And he's a terrific shot.'

The man laughs. 'Yes, yes! Rabbit every dinner!'

Later the man tells the boy that he is on his honeymoon. The boy does not say that he knows this already. The man explains that his wife is sleeping – he jerks his head upwards and sideways – in the room over there. She does not sleep well at night, he says. She needs – how do you say? – her *siesta*. She is a fellow teacher, the daughter of the headmaster of the school. She teaches art. A good artist, mainly watercolour.

Then the man leans forward, hands clasped between his knees, to ask: 'What is your name?'

'Evelyn.'

'Strange name! I never hear that name.'

'There was an English diarist. A long time ago. Evelyn. John Evelyn. My father was writing a book about him when I was born. '

'I am Götz.'

'Götz.' The boy likes the name. It has a monolithic solidity and strength that suit this stranger.

'You look German.'

'Me? German?' The boy is taken aback.

'Blue eyes. Blue, blue eyes. Like the sea. Like the Atlantic Ocean. And hair so blond. *Blond.*' Tentatively he extends a hand. Touches the hair briefly. Touches it again. Ruffles it.

A voice, high and querulous, calls: 'Götz!' It calls again. Something in German follows.

'*Meine Frau.* My wife. You will excuse.' He smiles. He puts a hand briefly on the boy's shoulder. Then he again ruffles the boy's hair, this time forcefully, almost aggressively. The boy's scalp tingles under the alien fingers, as though an electric shock were passing through it. 'Evelyn. Strange name. Good name. I like.' He smiles. Then he strides off to the far end of the balcony and enters the French windows into the room where his wife awaits him.

From then on their meetings are frequent but all too brief. The boy now spends most of his time reading on the balcony. He waits in patience. From time to time Götz appears, usually through the French windows. The chair still remains beside the boy's and Götz first stands briefly by it, leaning forward with a supporting hand on its back, and then sits on it. They have so much to say to each other, but all too often the high, querulous voice interrupts them. It seems to the boy that that cry of 'Götz, Götz!', usually followed by something in German, becomes increasingly plaintive, even desperate. Götz shrugs on one such occasion, then gives an embarrassed laugh as he puts a hand over the boy's and then hurriedly withdraws it: 'Women, women! Difficult!' He laughs as he gets to his feet. Again the woman calls: 'Götz! *Was machst du?*'

One evening after dinner, as the boy's mother fumbles over a Chopin nocturne on the out-of-tune piano and his brother, perched on the arm of a sagging sofa, flirts with the bosomy, red-cheeked daughter of the house seated on it, the boy gets up, his forefinger keeping his place in the book, and leaves the low-ceilinged room with its smells of omnipresent dust and of dead flowers left for far too long in a vase on a mantelpiece crowded with small objects and photographs in tarnished silver frames. There is a cramped hall outside the room. Beyond are three doors, one to the rooms in the main building, one out on to the balcony of the annexe and one to a lavatory. Götz is waiting in this small hall. The boy's first thought is that he is waiting there for him. Then he realises that, no, he must be waiting for his wife, who is in the lavatory. Götz smiles. He holds out his arms in invitation. The boy hesitates. Suddenly Götz lunges over and grabs him. In frenzied succession he presses his mouth to the side of the boy's neck, to his forehead, to his lips. The boy attempts to jerk away, then yields, at first reluctantly, then with an access of emotion that overpowers him like some huge breaker suddenly soaring skywards and then crashing downwards in a previously tranquil sea. There is a clank followed by the sound of flushing. The man retreats, pushing the boy away from him. The book falls from the boy's hand. He stoops. The German woman emerges. She stares at the boy, then at her husband. The boy notices that, though her face is, as always, coated with powder, there are raw, red patches on her bare arms and on one side of her throat.

Götz puts out a hand to the latch of the door that leads out to the balcony. He nods at the boy, then bows slightly as his wife, head lowered, passes out before him. He follows her without a backward glance.

The following day the German couple will leave. It is a long drive back to Düsseldorf. As Götz checks the car, a Mercedes but an old one, probably bought second hand, the boy's brother joins him. He is not interested in the Germans but he is interested in the car. He even helps to pump up a tyre. He then asks if he can have a quick spin. The German asks if he has a licence. He shakes his head. The German smiles and says: 'Sorry.' The boy wishes his brother would leave Götz alone. The farmer and his wife are angry with the brother because, unknown to them, he took their daughter to a bar in Han-sur-Lesse and brought her back in the early hours. The brother has described the girl as 'hot stuff' to the boy.

That night, almost at midnight, the boy creeps out of bed and, leaving his snoring brother sprawled across a sheet damp with sweat, tiptoes out on to the balcony. The night is stifling. In any case, he is in such a torment of emotion that he cannot sleep. He leans over the railing of the balcony and breathes in the air. But it does not cool him, even its breath is scorching. From far off a strange creaking sounds reaches him. A bird? An animal? There is something sinister, even frightening about the sound. It is like the creaking of a rocking chair hugely amplified. Behind him he hears another sound. He twists his body round. In the moonlight, wearing only his pyjamas, Götz puts a forefinger to his lips. Then he steps forward and takes the boy's hand in his. 'Come.'

At the farthest end of the balcony, there is a narrow, spiral staircase. The boy has never noticed it before, much less gone down it. Götz descends, crab-like, from time to time looking back over his shoulder. The boy follows, in unquestioning submission and wonder. Götz must have explored this region in preparation for what is now about to happen. There is a malodorous rubbish tip, surmounted by a broken sofa vomiting horsehair. There is a wheelbarrow without a wheel. There is a stack of old newspapers, blotched with damp and tied with hairy twine. In the extraordinarily bright light from the moon the boy can at once make out all these things. There is a door, with a glinting handle. Götz puts a sunburned hand with bitten nails to the handle and opens the door. He turns his head and smiles. There is an iron bedstead with a stained mattress on it.

Later Götz says, stooping to tie the cord of the boy's pyjama trousers with frowning attentiveness, as though for a child: 'It is only when I think of you that I can do it with her. Only then. And then it is still difficult.'

At the time these words seem to the boy a betrayal even more cruel than what has just happened on the bed.

Afterwards I asked for his address. At first he seemed reluctant to give it to me. 'I have no paper. You have paper?' I shook my head. 'Can you remember it?' 'I think so.' He told me the address, then repeated it. 'Say it,' he said. I said it. 'Perfect!' He laughed. 'Oh, Evelyn, I miss you, miss you!' The present tense made the utterance even more poignant. Our separation had already started.

'I'll write to you. Will you write to me?'

'Maybe.' Then he laughed: 'I make fun! Of course, if you write, I write! Yes, yes!'

'I'll tell you my address. Can you remember it?'

'No, no, you write letter first! My memory is bad!'

I stared at him. Then I took a step forward and grabbed his forearm, as though I were drowning and he were my rescuer. He stooped and for a last time put his lips to mine. 'It is only when I think of you – of you, only you – that I can do these things with her.' At that almost word-for-word repetition of what he had said only a short while before, I felt both triumph and a pang of desolation, but now none of that former guilt.

Because the journey was so long, they left early, at five in the morning. I woke and heard their voices, little more than whispers, as they dragged their luggage – so many and such large pieces! – down to the car. I swung my legs out of the bed and thought that I would go down to help them. Then I lay back on the bed again. If he had been alone, of course I would have gone down. But I did not want to see her or even think of her. When I thought of her, that poor creature with the thin arms and over-powdered face, I at once tried to think of him instead.

Eleven days later, the Germans invaded Poland. I wrote him letter after letter but none ever received an answer. His memory became like one of the snapshots taken by my mother during that Belgian holiday: shrivelling, yellowing, fading.

Two years after the War ended I attended a summer school at the university in Göttingen. There was a student from Girton in our party, beautiful, witty, sexually provocative, fluent in German. I thought that I was in love with her. 'I want to go to Düsseldorf to see if someone I knew before the War is still alive.' 'A German?' 'Yes. A German.' 'Well, why not?' In normal circumstances such travel would have been impossible. But no circumstances were normal for her and nothing was impossible. With the help of a titled cousin of hers, a colonel in the Control Commission, she fixed our weekend leave of absence from the summer school and the long, frequently interrupted journey across mile on mile of scorched, desolate landscape. She had insisted on coming with me – 'It'll be fun.'

Largely through her pertinacity and charm we eventually found first the street and then the house – with, next to it, a ruined building that had once been a school. It was in that ruined building that Götz and his wife must have taught. The house, their house, was also ruined. In London, where my mother and I had continued to live all through the Blitz, I had often viewed similar houses – their surfaces blackened, their contours broken and jagged, shreds of wall-paper cascading from their walls – with a mixture of dread and awe. I felt that dread and awe, in a far more intense form, now. Perhaps he had died there. I voiced that thought to my companion. 'Or somewhere,' she said, indifferent.

It was she who asked at the lodge at the gates of the ruined school. A shawled old woman, her mouth fallen in around the few front teeth that remained to her and her fingers grimy and greasy, answered our ringing of the bell. She squinted at us from under a ragged grey fringe, in what seemed to be both bewilderment and hostility. She did not know what had happened to the inhabitants of the house, she said. That was before her time. People had died, people had moved. She told us all this as though it had no interest for her.

I have just woken from another night of jumbled words, endlessly recurring, that I struggle now first to rescue from oblivion and then to arrange into some kind of sense. *The ladder upside down.* That odd phrase keeps repeating itself, like a bell tolling maddeningly on and on. I sip my coffee. I put a hand over my closed eyes and then press my fingers on to them until sparks shower downwards behind their lids. Yes, I begin to see what that strange phrase must mean. I reached the pinnacle of the ladder in that Belgian farmhouse before I had even started to climb it. The rest of my life became a descent, precarious rung by rung, until – now an old man no longer desired or even desirable – here I sit sipping coffee from a chipped cup in a kitchen that feels cold even though I have yet again turned up the central heating. *In my end is my beginning.* That phrase also now returns, a piece of flotsam on the reluctantly returning tide of memory. Then, as I did in my dream, I amend the sentence: *In my beginning was my end.* The most important thing that ever happened in my life ended when it had hardly begun.

'Evelyn!' It is my wife calling to me to remove her tray and help her to the bath. '*Evelyn!*' The tone of her voice, plaintive, even desperate, is uncannily like that of Götz's wife summoning him back to their bedroom more than sixty years ago. It is only by thinking of Götz – now either long since dead or a man even more ancient than myself – that I can continue to perform for her the tasks that I have to perform.

'Coming! I'm coming!'

The Sitting Tenant

Mark and Howard were an upwardly mobile couple in increasingly obsessive search of an upwardly mobile neighbourhood.

At first Dalston appealed to them. There were all those ethnic shops, restaurants and cafés, and, yes, all those Turks, with the sort of bristly moustaches that made Mark gasp with delight, even if they also made Howard groan with horror. Prices could only go up. During their prospecting, they were particularly taken with a straggly street of semi-detached Thirties houses. But then they noticed the black teenagers sprawled across a cracked rise of front-steps, while passing around a joint with indolent furtiveness. And, more serious, there was no underground to take Mark to the council office at which he worked or Howard to his dental surgery.

Acton? Acton was whizzing up. But there was something depressing about the quiet, even sombre streets, with so few people in them. Balham? A chum of theirs – well, more an acquaintance than a chum – had been mugged there when merely going out to buy some bananas in mid-afternoon. So, after a lot of discussion, they had decided, reluctantly, to rule Balham out.

Eventually, they opted for Stepney. It was a first view of Tredegar Square that clinched it. Oh, if only, if only! Mark, the older of the couple, who knew about such things, having once lived briefly and unhappily with a morose architect, was particularly enraptured. 'I love those giant recessed columns,' he sighed.

'Way beyond us.' Howard was always the practical one, apt to be tight when Mark was wanting to be generous.

'Yes, I know, sweetie, I know, don't I know! But one day ... That's what we're going to aim for.' Once again he gazed up at an elegant façade. 'You bet all the people living here are *very* grand. No council tenants.' His elderly parents still lived in a high-rise, much vandalised council block.

What clinched the matter was their finding of an estate agent who at once, as Mark put it, came up with the goods. 'Just call me Thelma – I hate formalities,' she told them at their first meeting. At that meeting she was already referring to them, flatteringly, as 'You boys'. Black and buxom, with a wide space between her front teeth and extremely long red fingernails, she at once adopted them as her friends. They reciprocated.

'I'm not sure how much this is going to appeal,' she told them at a second meeting after that first one had yielded 'nothing quite right'. 'It's just come in. You'll be the first people to view it.' It was a house unusually capacious for what, she had to admit, was still a neighbourhood largely occupied by Bangladeshis. Period. Well, Edwardian. The owner, an old lady, had had to go into a home, poor dear, after a stroke. The price was amazingly low for a property of that size, but that was because there were – 'I have to come clean to you boys' – two drawbacks that might put people off. Firstly, the old lady had let the house become a perfect tip. Secondly, there was a sitting tenant.

'A sitting tenant?' Mark pulled a face. He was good at faces.

'I'm not sure that I'm encouraged by that,' Howard said.

'Oh, he's a perfectly harmless old boy. A retired Army man – captain, major, I can't remember. I don't think you boys will have any trouble with him.'

'Well, let's take a dekko.'

'That's the spirit!' Thelma exclaimed, plunging downwards, arm outstretched, for her vast, red handbag and then lurching to her feet. 'It's a terrific bargain. And I don't think that the old chap is going to last all that long. You've only to look at him to realise that. On his last legs.'

Thelma panted up the uncarpeted stairs ahead of them. 'He has the attic area,' she explained superfluously between gasps. 'I'm afraid the higher and higher you climb, the worse and worse it gets.'

Mark did the face, expressing revulsion, that involved wrinkling his nose and pulling his upper lip upward and to one side. 'There's a distinct pong,' he said.

As they reached the final landing, both Mark and Howard were dismayed to discover that the tenant's quarters were not self-contained. There was a door open on to a lavatory, its linoleum worn here and there to holes. An ancient washbasin reared up in a corner. One pane of the dusty, cobwebbed window had been clumsily patched with cardboard now coming adrift at the edges.

Thelma rapped on a closed door beyond the open one. Silence. She rapped again. 'Major! Major Pomfrey.'

'Yes, yes. Come in. Come in!' The voice was high-pitched and nasal.

The major was seated on the edge of a narrow, unmade bed, with a half-smoked cigarette held at a jaunty angle between a forefinger and a middle finger amber from kippering with nicotine over many years. He was in striped flannel pyjamas, his feet, with their talon-like toenails, bare. 'Ah, Mrs Lucy. Good to see you. Forgive my dishabille. I overslept. A case of my alarm clock failing – not for the first time – to be alarming. Do sit.' There was one straight-backed chair, with a chamber pot, almost full to the brim, under it, and one armchair, over which some clothes were scattered.

The three intruders remained standing. 'We don't want to take up your time,' Thelma said. 'But, as I explained on the blower, these are the two possible purchasers of the house. They just wanted to say a hello to you.'

'They'll be fools to buy this place. Falling down. Rising damp in the basement and ground floor. Cockroaches. Mice. Even rats.'

'Now come on, major, it's not as bad as all that,' Thelma chided, not attempting to conceal her annoyance that he should at once start to run down a property that she had had every hope of selling. 'Well, let me introduce...'

The major extended a shaky hand but did not get up. As Howard took the hand, he noticed, with distaste, the orange urine stain in the crotch of the major's pyjamas. He, not Mark, was the one who noticed such things.

'Have you been here long?' Mark asked.

'Thirty-two years. Moved here when I lost some money through a daft investment – and my wife died. Two disasters together. Within a month of each other.' He stared fixedly up at Mark with pale blue eyes that suddenly had a glitter of malevolence in them. 'Sitting tenant. Can't be put out. Controlled rent.'

'Yes, we know that,' Howard said. 'I don't see why that should be a difficulty'

'The old girl tried to get me out. Many times. At one point even cut off the electricity. Never had any luck!' He laughed. 'You won't either.'

After the brief meeting, Mark and Howard invited Thelma to a cup of coffee at the Starbucks opposite to her office.

'I don't think he'll really pose any problem,' Thelma said.

'I noticed that he didn't have a television set,' Howard said. 'Or a hi-fi. So there'd be no arguments over noise.'

'We hate noise,' Mark said. 'Unless we ourselves are making it,' he added with a laugh.

'The house definitely has possibilities.' Howard raised his cup of *latte* and sipped daintily.

'It's an absolute snip,' Mark said. 'I can already see in my mind's eye what we could do with it.'

Thelma wondered whether to mention that, although the sitting tenant had his own lavatory and washbasin, he had no bathroom and was entitled, by a long-standing agreement, to use the downstairs one. She decided not to. After all, it didn't look as if the old boy took a bath all that often.

'Well, you boys must have a good think. I don't want to rush you. But I must tell you, I'm showing round two other interested parties tomorrow.'

'Then we'll have to get our skates on,' Howard said.

'But don't let's rush things,' Mark warned. Howard was so impulsive.

Howard was often kept late at the surgery. Much of the decorating therefore fell to Mark, even though, as he was the first to acknowledge, he was not the practical one of the two and in any case had a bad back. There were, of course, things that even Howard could not do, and so, though constantly anxious about the rising costs of repairs on top of monthly payments on a substantial mortgage, the couple from time to time had to call in two jolly black builders recommended by Thelma, whose cousins they were.

From the start, the major was all too obviously fascinated by the work going on below him. Usually wearing nothing more than those striped, flannel pyjamas and slippers, he would slowly descend the creaking stairs, crab-wise, a hand clutching the banisters, and then position himself in a corner of whatever room in which work was in progress. Leaning against the wall, emaciated arms akimbo, he would stare fixedly for a long time before finally making some suggestion or criticism, more often the latter – 'You've got some of that paint smeared on the wainscot', 'That nail's not straight', 'Here, here! Hold on! Hold on! You've forgotten that spot over there.' These interventions unnerved Mark and Howard, who then became even clumsier. They infuriated the builders, who eventually gave an ultimatum – 'That geezer's got to leave us alone or we quit.'

It was Howard, the more diplomatic of the two, to whom devolved the task of telling the major that work would proceed more smoothly if he did not interfere.

'Oh, dear! Oh-dear-oh-dear! Well, now isn't that sad? So-o-o sad!' The high, pinched voice was sarcastic. 'I'd hate to put you off your stroke. What a sensitive couple you are, aren't you?'

'It's the builders too.'

'The *builders*? Oh, you mean the cowboys. Did I tell you that I saw one of them pinching a packet of your biscuits? Chocolate Bourbons. I glimpsed him opening the top drawer of that cupboard in your kitchen, when he didn't know I could see him from the hall.' He chuckled. 'It's amazing how dark-skinned people are so often light-fingered.'

At first Mark and Howard, who were genuinely kind and tolerant, did their best to accommodate 'Pomme Frite' (as they had soon nicknamed Major Pomfrey). They told each other that, with his innumerable prejudices, he was a figure from the past; that, with his wife long since dead and his estranged daughter, the only child of the marriage, far away in New Zealand, the poor creature was desperately lonely; that one had to remember that he was suffering from a host of ailments, ranging from the bronchial cough that reverberated through the house at daybreak every morning with all the regularity of a rooster, to the diabetes for which he had to give himself a daily injection. One could not really be unfriendly, much less hostile, to someone so pathetic.

But over the ensuing months Pomme Frite's intrusions became less and less supportable. Soon after they had moved in, he had asked them whether – since his television set had broken down and he was 'too old to go to all the bother and expense of getting another so late in the day' – they would mind if he watched the cricket on theirs when they were out at work. Reluctantly they had acceded. Entering the sitting-room that evening, after a day of hard work, they sniffed angrily at an unpleasant combination of cigarette smoke and urine, before one of them rushed to fling up the windows and the other frantically busied himself with emptying the overflowing ashtray.

Then something even more appalling happened. They were seated before the television set one evening, watching *Who Wants to be a Millionaire?*, when Pomme Frite's head appeared around the door. 'Would you mind awfully if I joined you?' Without waiting for a response, he began to nudge a chair forward with a bony knee. Eventually, unable to stand the alien presence any longer, Mark exclaimed: 'Oh, this is a bore!', jumped up and switched off the set. 'Yes, we ought to be thinking about our supper,' Howard chimed in. But a few evenings later, Pomme Frite once again joined them, clutching a packet of cigarettes and a lighter against his narrow, bony chest, even though they had by then made it amply clear that they could not abide smoking.

Pomme Frite had a way of usurping the bathroom just when they themselves wished to use it before rushing out to work or a party. Eventually, exasperated beyond endurance by the sound of water constantly running at their expense with a counterpoint of coughing and violent expectoration, they suggested that it might be more convenient for all three of them if they agreed on fixed hours when the bathroom would be at his sole disposal. To that Pomme Frite responded: 'Oh, lordy, lordy! You two spend *hours* there, while yours truly waits around, sponge-bag and shaving kit at the ready. One might be living with two members of the fairer sex from the time that you take. No, no, I don't think it would be a good idea to fix definite times. I'll just go on slipping in whenever you give me the chance.'

Soon the intrusions extended to the kitchen. 'I hope you won't take it amiss. I suddenly found that I had run out of bread and so, transgressing on your good natures, I helped myself to two of those ciabatta rolls that I found in your bread bin. Rather past their sell-by date, but any port in a storm.' Seeing the look of indignation on the two faces opposite, he replied huffily: 'Of course I'll replace them. Though not perhaps with products quite so recherché.' He never did replace them. A short while later, when, having for once returned early from work, Howard went into the kitchen to make himself some coffee, he was exasperated to find a saucepan tilted sideways on the range, its sides clogged with a dark-grey deposit, so obstinate that he had to take a Brillo pad to it. He decided that it was the remains of a custard left over from the previous night. Pomme Frite must have succeeded in burning it while heating it up for his own consumption,

At first Mark and Howard had been concerned about the diabetes. One day, returning from one of his rare forays to the local Wop shop (as he called it), Pomme Frite had staggered through the front door, leaving it wide open, and had then collapsed on to the bottom of the staircase. Fortunately Howard returned home a few minutes later. 'My syringe, syringe. Medicine cupboard. In the WC. ' Howard raced upstairs, opened the rusty, dusty medicine cupboard, and found a disposable syringe and a phial of insulin. Later, Pomme Frite croaked 'You saved my bloody life. Not that it was worth saving,' he added. 'You're a good chap. Basically.' Laughter caused his bony shoulders to shake up and down. 'Even if you're a queer one.'

Did that last sentence mean what Howard and Mark thought that it meant? At that stage in the relationship they could not be sure.

Later, they were. The two of them were having one of their intermittent spats in the hall, over an invitation that each of them thought that the other had agreed to answer, when from above them they heard that disgustingly phlegmy cough and then the high-pitched, nasal voice: 'Girls! Girls! Please! Why not give each other a nice kiss and make up?' Pomme Frite was leaning over the banister, his face a grey disk in the gloom of the attic landing.

When they next had a party, it was clear that Pomme Frite had similarly been surveying the arrivals – and perhaps also the departures – of the guests from above. 'What an interesting crowd,' he commented to Mark the next morning, at the end of a breathless struggle to pick up some letters off the doormat. None of the letters was for him. Having carefully scrutinised each in turn, he held out the pile. 'I was hoping to see some popsies, but all I saw ... Well, one lives and learns. This has become an odd old world. You two have certainly brought me up to date with a bump.'

A few days later, the old man and Mark coincided outside the bathroom. Mark was wearing a polo-necked cashmere sweater just bought at the Harrod's sale. Mockingly Pomme Frite looked him up and down. 'Well, you look very saucy in that little number, I must say,' he announced in what sounded like a feeble imitation of Graham Norton. Certainly Mark had wondered if that pale blue shade was quite right for him, but to be told, at the age of forty-seven and in line for promotion to the head of refuse collection, that he looked 'saucy' was bloody cheek.

Somehow these oblique aspersions on their sexuality exasperated Mark and Howard more acutely than any of the more flagrant outrages. It was, in fact, those aspersions that finally persuaded them to try to bribe Pomme Frite to leave – ill though they could afford to do so after all the money that they had had to spend on the house.

As so often, it was Howard who was the spokesman. He entered the low-ceilinged attic room, his tall, thin body leaning slightly forward, as so often when he wished to ingratiate himself. 'Am I disturbing you?'

'No, no! Liberty hall. Take a pew.'

Without taking a pew, Howard produced the spiel that he and Mark and had prepared together. They were worried that their tenant was isolated up so many stairs. They were also worried that he might fall ill while they were both out at work. Had he thought that it might be better if he applied to the Council for sheltered housing?

'I can't say that I have. No. I'm perfectly happy here. You two do so much to look after me.'

'If you did decide to go, we'd be only too happy to – to – well, make a contribution.'

'A contribution? What sort of contribution?'

'Well, five thousand or so.'

'*Five thousand*?'

Useless.

'He's like those cockroaches,' Mark said. 'Quite disgusting. And amazingly persistent.'

'If only we could stamp him out of existence, as we did them.'

'It wasn't the stamping that finally got rid of them. It was that pest control officer.'

'I don't suppose that the Council employs a human pest control officer. That gas was awfully effective.'

Looking back later, each of them decided that that was the moment when the idea first began to germinate. But neither ever confessed that to the other.

Howard came home early with a feverish cold and, having made himself a pot of tea, got into his pyjamas and prepared to clamber into his bed. It was then that he noticed that the bedside radio had vanished. It was not the first time that Pomme Frite had borrowed it, his own ancient Roberts set having expired two or three weeks previously. Howard pulled on his dressing gown, thrust his feet into his slippers, and strode out into the hall. From above he could hear the blare, imperfectly tuned in, of a Sousa march. Taking them in twos and threes, he raced up the stairs.

He banged on the attic door and eventually, getting no answer, flung it open. 'You really have a cheek —' he began. Then he saw the emaciated body, naked except for some underpants, lying sideways across the bed. It was like a gigantic, grey grub, he often used to recall in horror in later days. Pomme Frite's mouth was open. Without the false teeth, it contained only two jagged, orange-black fangs. There was a whistling sound of air being drawn in and then expelled. The prominent adam's apple bobbed up and down.

Howard began to dash to the lavatory medicine cupboard. As a dentist, he was used to giving injections. No sweat. But then he hesitated, turned back and re-entered the room. He stared down at the grub. He could leave Pomme Frite there, in the hope that the diabetic coma would be a fatal one. Or else...? He picked up the pillow in its soiled case, from where it had tumbled to the floor. He cradled it for a moment, like a baby, in the crook of an arm. Then, with a decisive movement, he put it over Pomme Frite's face. The grey body stirred, frantically twitched from side to side. The tassel penis dribbled some urine. With sudden ferocity — better to be safe than sorry — Howard jumped on to the pillow and bounced up and down on it. After that, everything was over quickly. He went downstairs, put on the clothes so recently taken off, and let himself out into the street. His feverish cold seemed miraculously to have cured itself. He decided to go to the gym, where on his last visit he had got into conversation with a muscular Bangladeshi attendant. Promising, very promising.

★

Pomme Frite's death brought with it three surprises.

Firstly, there was the surprise of the size of his estate: £626,000. 'And to think that we thought that the old brute was on the verge of destitution!' was Howard's comment.

Secondly, there was the surprise of what he wrote in his will about his bequest to Mark and Howard: *I had expected an increasingly lonely and unhappy old age. But the purchase of the house by these two gentlemen has totally changed my life. Since they took over the house, I have felt that I once more belong to a family. They have been like two sons to me.*

Thirdly there was the surprise that the bequest to Mark and Howard consisted of the whole of Pomme Frite's estate.

Mark and Howard, their Renault loaded with the few possessions not taken by the removers the day before, drove towards Tredegar Square. They had sold the horrid old house to a young, spruce, Vietnamese couple, owners of a successful restaurant, with a large brood of children, for a sum almost twice what they had paid for it. They had haggled over the house in Tredegar Square with its ancient, upper-crusty owners, all but been gazumped, and then emerged victorious.

'I think this is the happiest day of my life,' Howard said.

'Happier than the one on which we first met?' That had been on Hampstead Heath.

'Well, no, not quite,' Howard remarked untruthfully. 'But almost.'

'Tredegar Square – here we come!'

Mark looked across the Square, to those giant recessed columns, with proprietary love. Then he gasped, pointed. 'Who – who is that?'

Howard craned his neck, gripping the steering wheel. A hand was raising the net curtain of one of the two attic rooms. Then, with horror and incredulity, both of them made out the figure in the striped flannel pyjamas.

The sitting tenant had arrived ahead of them.

Causes

1

She is a tall, emaciated, middle-aged American woman with a heavy jaw, a high, sloping forehead and an unhealthily yellow skin. She is a painter, I remember from what my twin sister Maria once wrote to me. But if these views of feluccas under full sail on the Nile, donkeys tethered beside picturesque wells and minarets against lurid sunsets are examples of her work, then she isn't a good one. Her Egyptian husband is out on business, she has told me.

'You must be tired.' She holds out a cup of tea.

'Yes.' I sigh. 'I had to set off so early and we took so much longer to get here than I'd expected. That's always the problem with bargain flights.'

'It was I who found her. An awful shock. There'd been no sign of illness – except that her memory was going. In fact, she'd been helping me plant some vegetables only two or three days before it happened. As you know of course, she loved to garden.'

'She told me more than once how kind you'd been to her.'

'Well, we were sorry for her. She seemed to be so alone.' Am I right in sensing an oblique reproach? 'And of course we were fond of her too. She was a darling – in that rather eccentric way of hers. She was a woman of causes. That's how I always thought of her. A woman of causes. She was addicted to causes in the same way that my husband is addicted to

173

cigarettes. Both dangerous things in the long run. It's all right to battle for causes in your country or in mine, but in a country like Egypt...' She raises her mug in both hands and sips from it. 'That was one of the reasons that we persuaded her to leave Cairo for Luxor.' She smiles in sad reminiscence. 'There was less chance of her getting up to any kind of mischief. She once told me she was sure her 'phone was being tapped – and her mail being opened.'

'Perhaps that's why she so seldom answered my letters. Perhaps my letters never got to her.'

'She loved hearing from you. But she knew how busy you were.'

I feel an irrational urge to defend myself. I want to say: 'You know, I never forgot her. Or neglected her. But if I sent her money – which I could often ill afford – I knew she'd spend it not on herself but on some hare-brained crusade or one of the lame dogs that always ended up by biting her. The sad thing was that she spent all her time battling for strangers, many of them worthless or wicked, while we of her family ... She didn't even return to England when our mother was dying.' But what would be the point?

'What we admired most about her was her courage. She was afraid of no one – nothing. When they were about to execute the man who threw the bomb at that busload of tourists, she even stood for hours on end outside the house of the minister for home affairs with a loud speaker and a placard. Typically she had failed to discover that he wasn't there. When she repeatedly refused to move on, they finally arrested her. That was when my husband and I thought it best to get her out of Cairo. So we offered her the shack. That's what we call it, the shack. It's a bungalow that we built next to this house for my mother. But my mother took one look at it and returned to Maine. So Maria became a kind of substitute mother to me.' She peers at me. 'You were twins, weren't you?'

I nod.

'One would never guess it.' It's what people have said ever since we were children together out in India. 'You're so unlike. In every way.'

I look out of the window at the wide, tawny, slow-moving river. A felucca is tacking from this bank, the west, to the other. Its wake glitters in the afternoon sunlight. I feel a sudden, ineluctable weariness.

She must have sensed this. 'Would you like to lie down before you start on things?'

Now that I am in my eighties, people are constantly asking me if I'd like to lie down. I shake my head. 'No. Thank you. I'm all right. It's the change of temperature more than anything else.'

She laughs: 'For us today is *cool*!'

Having finished my cup of tea and refused a second one, I get up and out of politeness wander round the room, inspecting the pictures.

She surprises me by saying: 'They're not much good, I'm afraid. But the tourists buy them. And that helps with the bills. My husband's travel business isn't doing well. No travel business is. That's because of the political situation, of course.'

Eventually she takes me across to what she has called the shack. A square concrete box, with a roof of rusty corrugated iron, it's extremely ugly. But Maria would never have noticed that. Once, when I spoke disparagingly of some stark council blocks near to the poky rented flat in which she was then living in Peckham, she retorted angrily: 'The disadvantaged can't afford the luxury of beauty. And so beauty doesn't interest them.' 'Disadvantaged' was a word she often used.

'I've put out a lot of boxes and plastic bags for you.'

'You're very kind.'

'As you can see, the room is a mess. Once I tidied it for her when she was out. She was furious. So that was the last time I dared to do that.'

'Every place in which she ever lived was a mess.' I might have added: 'As was her life.'

She puts a hand to the dead irises in a glass vase, the water dank and dark, that rests on a table among piles of dog-eared books and magazines. Petals flake off and drift downwards. 'If I can help in any way ... '

'You're very kind. But I think it'll be best if I tackle all this alone. I'll just do as much I can today and then, if there's still more to be done, perhaps you won't mind –'

'Of course not. Take your time. Just shout if you need anything. I'm not planning to go out. I must finish off a daub.' She laughs. 'A commission, believe it or not.'

She shuts the door behind her. There is an unpleasant smell, sour and yet also cloyingly sweet, of urine in the room. I try to expel it from my consciousness but cannot do so. I look around me. On the rickety table by the narrow, iron bedstead there is a photograph that I recognise as being of Fidel Castro, not as he is now but as he was soon after the revolution. He looks handsome, proud, petulant. Maria was a frequent visitor to Cuba when few other people ever ventured there. On more than one occasion she met him. He has signed the photograph for her. She must have treasured it through the years of constant, erratic travel and of restless moving from one bedsit or tiny flat to another. Typical of her never to have bought a frame, however cheap, for a possession so important to her. For lack of protection, the photograph has yellowed at the corners and has a crumpled look to it. I hold it up, stare at it and then replace it. I pull open a drawer. It is full of stockings rolled into balls, handkerchiefs, vests, knickers, cotton blouses. Nothing has been ironed. Clearly some things have not been washed.

I feel an overwhelming sadness. I also once again feel that ineluctable tiredness that makes every movement – even the pushing back of the drawer – a superhuman effort. With a sigh I fall on to her bed. As children in India, sharing a room, we would often creep into each other's beds. This bed is unforgivingly hard and the one pillow feels as if it were stuffed with straw. It as on this bed that the American woman – Mrs Bird, Bard, Baird, I cannot remember – must have found her. But surprisingly the thought of her lifeless body lying there does not fill me with horror or revulsion. It is even comforting, though I can smell carbolic and can also still smell that sour-sweet urine stench.

I put a hand to my forehead. I shut my eyes. When one is very old, as I am, reality and dreams blur into each other. Simultaneously one sleeps and one is awake, as though one were two people. The present becomes a feather-light dream, the past an oppressive reality …

2

….The first thing that I noticed was the shoes. Clearly they had once been elegant. But now their former white was scratched, scuffed and discoloured in patches, and each was trodden down at the heel. One shoelace was white but a length of twine did service for the other. The reason that I saw the shoes before I saw the face of the man who was wearing them was that I was squatting in the dust as I wound up the model aeroplane that my father and mother had recently given me for my eighth birthday. The task involved rotating the propeller of the flimsy, balsa-wood biplane between thumb and forefinger until the elastic was taut. When I had completed the task, I jumped to my feet, plane in hand, and launched it out over the garden. My mother and the owner of the shoes both broke off their conversation, and my twin sister, Maria, who had been squatting beside me, intently watching what I had been doing, jumped to her feet. We all gazed skywards and then raised our hands to shield our eyes against the glare. I felt an intense, transient joy as the small, indomitable object moved erratically across the yellow-brown lawn and then spiralled down into a rose-bed choked with weeds.

Sharing my joy, Maria clapped her hands.

My mother turned back to the man.

His present name was Joseph, but once it had been Rasipuram, he was later to tell us. He had become Joseph when he had been converted to Christianity at a Lucknow mission school. At the age of eleven he had been admitted to the school not merely as a pupil but also to work as a part-time kitchen hand in lieu of the fees that neither he nor his family could pay. He had arrived at our house, hundreds of miles from Lucknow, and now he was looking for work. My father was also a missionary, and a member of his congregation had told Joseph that our cook had returned to his Himalayan village because of the illness of his wife and that we were looking for another cook. It was this job that Joseph wanted.

My sister, always eager to be my acolyte, raced off to fetch the model plane. I now stood behind the man, listening to what passed between him and my mother. When I had looked up from the white shoes, I had felt an immediate attraction, I do not know why. Short, mahogany-skinned and muscular, he was dressed in tattered khaki trousers and grubby white shirt. His hair, reaching to his shoulders, was ebony and shiny in the sunlight. The line of the jaw was strong. Later, when he finally turned away, his errand successfully accomplished, I saw the square face, with a puckered scar on the forehead, a nose that was all but flat, and soft, dark eyes.

After all her years in India, my mother still spoke only rudimentary Hindi. The man's English – because of the time that he had spent at the mission school, he said – was far, far better. It was therefore in English that they talked while I – and later my sister, the aeroplane cupped in both her hands as though it were a bird – listened.

'Have you any experience as a cook?'

'Oh, yes, lady. I was assistant to cook at other mission. I learn everything from him.'

'The sahib is fussy about his food. He isn't easy to please. About what he eats, I mean.' So ascetic in all other respects, my father was a constant, almost neurotic complainer about the meals served to him. Of all the luxuries of his previous life in England, good food remained the only one now important to him.

'I am sure I can please the sahib. I can learn.'

In the event, my mother, herself an excellent cook, found him the aptest of pupils. He was also, unlike our previous cook, as obsessive as my mother about hygiene. About that previous cook my mother often told a story to illustrate how 'impossible' (invariably her word when on the subject, a favourite of hers) Indian servants could be. At a dinner-party for the Governor, then on a visit to the city, and some prominent members of the English community, there had been an interminable wait for the main course, leg of lamb. My mother had eventually excused herself and hurried along to the kitchen. She had there found the cook squatting on the floor, with the bone of one of the two legs of lamb clasped between big toe and the one next to it as he struggled to carve the far too tough meat with a knife far too blunt. Slices were falling on to the grimy floor. My mother had hesitated and had then decided that, since there was no alternative, the lamb had better be served up to the guests.

With Joseph everything perishable would be stored away in the larder or the giant icebox, the flypapers would be constantly renewed, and stacks of dirty crockery no longer waited to be washed from one meal or even one day to another, as in the past. Joseph, my mother would often say, was a treasure.

My father, too, approved of him. He could scramble eggs exactly as my father insisted on having them, neither too watery nor too dry, his puff pastry was miraculously light, and he always used boiling water to make the China (never Indian) tea of which my father drank so much. From time to time, seated at his desk while, hands clasped before him, Joseph stood respectfully in front of him, my father would start some religious conversation of a kind that my mother, if she was present, would soon find a way to terminate. Poor Joseph could find no such way. 'I have been thinking of the Gaderene swine,' I heard my father begin on one occasion. On another it was: 'Have you ever wondered when reading of the

Prodigal Son...?' He was a genuinely religious and decent man, constantly tormented by the mysteries both of the Bible and of the faith that he painfully and persistently tried to derive from it. He was also an excellent doctor, with the natural flair for diagnosis essential for success in those days when scientific tests were far fewer and more fallible.

My mother assigned to Joseph what was no more than a mud hut in the servants' quarters. Instead of a door it had a curtain improvised from a tattered, gaudily striped green-and-orange bedspread, Indian in manufacture, that had once covered the bed of a nanny who had long since left us. There were two bungalows between ours – the one closest to the toy church, with its perfunctory gothic ornamentation and crooked spire – and the gate to the compound. In one of the other bungalows lived Dr Penrose, the grey, grim, childless head of the mission, inconsolable for the loss of his wife to typhoid, and in the other the young, recently married couple, the Roches, with the ready smiles and the Geordie accents, who had arrived only a few weeks before. The couple, along with my mother, conducted lessons in the little, airless hall behind the church.

The children of other English families with which we from time to time exchanged visits were forbidden by their parents to go near any servant quarters, theirs or anyone else's, much less to enter them. But, highly unusual for that era, our parents had no qualms about our doing so. They were a couple without any racial prejudice. My mother's severe judgements were directed impartially at white and brown alike, and my father made absolutely no differentiation of treatment between his many Indian patients and his few European or American ones.

However, both my parents retained the acute sense of class distinction imbued in them – my mother the daughter of a baronet with a small country estate, my father the son of a successful barrister – from their earliest years. Among their closest friends were a grand Indian couple who lived in a rambling house, not unlike some Victorian vicarage in a wealthy parish in England, called, despite its relatively modest size, 'The Palace'. The man, who had been educated at Harrow and Oxford, would have been the maharajah of a small state if his grandfather had not abdicated on becoming a Christian. To Indians not of this sort of standing, my parents were always courteous and friendly; but their attitude remained essentially one of superiors to inferiors and patrons to protégés. Such people were never among their dinner guests, just as their equivalents would never have been their dinner guests back in England.

Maria and I had already been in the habit of visiting the servants' quarters even before Joseph's arrival. Now we went there frequently. I used to feel an inexplicable excitement as, without declaring my presence before doing so, I jerked aside the old bedspread and entered, followed by Maria. Often, for want of a chair, Joseph would be squatting or reclining on the narrow, low bedstead, which, unlike our two beds, did not have springs but, instead, horizontal and vertical cords interwoven in a criss-cross pattern. He always seemed to be happy to see us, putting down the book or newspaper that he had been reading and simultaneously screwing up his eyes and smiling up at us as his face caught the sunlight all at once introduced by my raising of the improvised curtain.

Although, at the age of eight, both of us were now avid readers, I was curiously uninterested in the books, usually written in English, that he would hold up to show us. But Maria would glance at them and sometimes even read a page or two. Many years later, when we were in our thirties, she told me that one of these books had been Carlyle's *Latter-Day Pamphlets* and another the first volume of *Das Kapital* in an English translation. Could that have been true? She had a gift not merely for causes but also for misremembering.

As soon as we had returned from school – to which an elderly orderly would take us and bring us back – we would often rush over to Joseph's quarters to see if he were there. By then my parents would have had their lunch and my mother, never my father, would be having what she called 'a little lie-down'. Joseph would be free. Maria would sit on the bed beside him and I would squat on the mud floor. Later my mother would chide me 'The seat of those shorts is filthy! What have you been doing?' Joseph told us that he had learned to play the recorder at the previous mission. He would now pick up the instrument set out, together with his few books, his turban and his pair of white shoes (given to him, he had by now told us, by one of the missionaries) on a page of *The Times of India* in one corner of his room. On it he would play to us. At the time there seemed to me nothing incongruous in hearing him play 'The Blue Bells of Scotland' or 'Greensleeves', two staples of his repertoire. I can never hear either of those tunes now without a mingled feeling of longing, sadness and bewilderment.

Something else that Joseph told us that he had learned at the previous mission was woodcarving. He would do this with a two-bladed penknife, working deftly and quickly on wood that he foraged from the trees in our compound. Sometimes we would ourselves bring him suitable pieces of wood. The objects that he produced were usually animals – cats, dogs, bullocks, donkeys – crude and showing no particular skill but easily recognisable. At Christmas he produced some diminutive sheep and cattle for the crib that my mother would set up each year. Some of these objects he would present to us, some to other members of the mission or to friends of ours.

On the bed, Maria had a way of sitting extremely close to him. She would even lean against him, her face upturned as he talked or played to us. Occasionally he would put an arm around her shoulders, pulling her even closer. Then an expression of dreamily abstracted happiness would appear on her face, and she would shut her eyes, as if about to go to sleep. Even my parents might have disapproved of this proximity between their daughter and a servant. Our British and American neighbours would certainly have done so. But to me, at that age, it seemed in no way odd, much less an occasion for disapproval or alarm.

I rarely visited Joseph in the kitchen but Maria often did so. Soon she had become both his part-time assistant and his pupil. He instructed her in how to thicken gravy, make a *roux,* poach an egg, prepare vegetables. She could have learned all these things from our mother but she preferred to learn them only from him. Divinity fudge, always tricky, was a speciality of our mother. But it was from Joseph that Maria acquired a skill in making it that remained with her into old age. On the rare occasions when she came to stay with me, she would announce 'I think I'm going to make you some divinity fudge' and my heart would then sink. She would leave the kitchen in a mess that affronted my natural tidiness, with the pan often burned. Worse, having loved the glistening mini-peaks of peppermint-flavoured sugar and white of egg as a child, I now hated an excessive sweetness that made my teeth ache.

Maria, unlike myself, had never been a docile child. But she always did precisely what Joseph told her. Once she said to me: 'Oh, I do wish Joseph were younger!' 'Why?' 'Because then I could marry him when I grow up.' 'Oh, that would be no good! He's so poor.' 'I don't care.'

In March, as the temperature began to rise and rise and my mother and father debated whether she should or should not take us both up to

181

Naini Tal, leaving him to suffer the hot weather on his own, Maria and I celebrated our joint ninth birthday. On both that day and the day before it Joseph would allow neither of us into his kitchen. He was preparing a surprise for us, he told us. We guessed what the surprise would be. It would be roast chicken with sage and onion stuffing, bread sauce, roast potatoes and tinned peas. Chicken was our favourite dish.

Chicken it was, when we sat down for lunch on that Saturday. 'Joseph's bread sauce is better than mine,' our mother said, admiringly but not wholly pleased.

'You've made him into a first-rate cook,' my father said.

'He has a natural talent. That Ahmed was beyond any teaching.'

'Oh, don't talk of Ahmed. I often thought he'd poison me with that filthy kitchen and the flies and the ice-box dripping water.'

At the end of the meal our mother announced: 'Now we have Joseph's surprise.' She got up and went out to the kitchen.

We knew from previous birthdays what we would hear next. From far down the corridor between the kitchen and dining room we heard her strong, not always accurate contralto:

Happy birthday to you

Happy birthday to you

Happy birthday, dear children,

Happy birthday to you...

Then Joseph was singing, in a nasal, no less loud tenor. Maria and I giggled, not in mockery, but in surprise and pleasure. He entered the room first, carrying the large, murderous knife that we so often watched him sharpening, sparks whirling away from the whetstone, when we were to have a Sunday joint. Behind came my mother, bearing a huge cake, the flames of its eighteen candles, nine for Maria, nine for me, juddering in the dry, dust-laden wind that had been blowing in through the open window.

She set down the cake with a sigh. Her forehead was damp, straying hairs sticking to it. 'There you are, children! Look what Joseph has prepared for you!'

Maria pointed: 'Us! *Us!* They're us.'

Joseph had carved two figures, standing close to each other, their arms intertwined. One was a boy, dressed in white shorts and a blue, short-sleeved shirt, just like ones that I often wore. The other was a girl in a gym-tunic with black strap shoes fashioned not out of leather but some sort of black cloth. The two figures were inseparable, we later discovered, carved from a singe piece of wood.

Maria's eyes glittered in the light of the candles. Her mouth was open, as though she were about to cry out. I, too, stared transfixed.

'Isn't that lovely?' our mother said. 'Oh, Joseph, you've been to so much trouble. You shouldn't have! You *shouldn't* have!'

Later, we quarrelled about who was to keep the conjoined figures. I think that we both felt, though we would never say it, that they were symbolic of the lives that we had shared so closely. We did then not realise how soon and abruptly those lives would be separated, as though someone had taken an axe to the figures, splitting the single piece of wood into two. We were doomed to become remittance children, like thousands and thousands of others packed off 'home', to be looked after by relatives, friends or even total strangers. I would go to an uncle and aunt, who already had a brood of six brats and certainly did not welcome another. Maria would go to our German grandmother in Switzerland, where she would be cosseted and indulged. We would rarely see each other again until the war was over and we were past twenty.

'I'm older than he is. So I should have them,' Maria said.

'But I'm the *boy*!' I shouted. 'Anyway she's only twenty minutes older.'

'He likes me better. Joseph likes me better.'

'Liar!'

'If I were Solomon I'd cut that piece of wood in two,' our father said.

'Why don't you toss for it?' my mother proposed.

Reluctantly we agreed.

Maria won, as she usually did when we tossed for anything.

She looked at me, worried and sad. 'I'm sorry,' she said. Suddenly she held out the figures. 'You have them if you want. I don't mind.'

I shook my head. It was not the first time that it was brought home to me that she had a far more generous nature than I had.

It was two or three weeks later that the unbelievable thing happened. With its abruptness and horror it might have been a car crash or train crash or an attack of the cholera that had been reported to be spreading in the native quarter.

It was yet another unbearably hot day. On the one following it, after repeated changes of mind, my mother had resolved at last to take Maria and me up into the hills of Naini Tal. Two electric fans were whirring at either end of the dining-room. The windows were closed, as they now always were until the scorching air outside had begun to cool with the sinking of the sun. Our bearer was on holiday and so it was Joseph's assistant, the *kitmatgar*, little more than a boy with the vestige of a moustache above his long, thin upper lip, who staggered in with an overloaded tray bearing our lunch. From time to time, either my mother or father would say 'We really must get a trolley' but neither did anything about it.

My mother leaned across the table and picked up the cut-glass jug containing filtered water. A lace doiley, fringed with beads, covered it. She jerked off the doiley. 'Who's for water?' She and my father never drank alcohol, even though they always provided it for their guests. My father held out his glass. Meantime, the boy began to unload his tray. My father loved curry, as he also loved the sticky Indian sweets that most westerners abhorred. He also liked his curry to be extremely hot, which my mother, my sister and I certainly did not. As a result whenever we had curry, as on this Sunday, Joseph prepared two different dishes, one mild for us and one hot for him. The boy set down before my mother the silver entrée dish, with the crest of her family on it, containing the one curry. He set down the other curry, also in a similar entrée dish, before my father. My father, who, even on that Sunday, had from the early hours been visiting patients too ill to come to his surgery, was ravenous, as always. He grabbed a serving spoon and, plate in hand, dug out some rice from another dish, placed equidistant from all of us in the centre of the table. Then he piled two spoonfuls of his curry on top of it.

'Mango chutney?' my mother asked, herself taking up a spoon.

Reluctant to open his mouth for any purpose other than eating, my father merely shook his head. He never took chutney, as the rest of us did, but my mother nonetheless always offered it to him.

He piled a fork high with rice and curry, raised it to his mouth and swallowed greedily. Then he again began to pile the fork high. Suddenly he gagged, put a hand to his throat and began to gasp and snort, his eyelids fluttering. My mother leaped to her feet, knocking back her chair, and raced round the table. Later, she was to say that she thought that he was having a stroke. It was from a stroke that she had seen her father die when she was still a child. 'What is it? What's the matter?'

Stupefied, Maria and I remained seated, staring in amazement and terror.

Suddenly my father began to vomit, with an astonishing, projectile force. A particularly violent spasm caused him to topple from his chair, with a resounding crash.

As always in an emergency, my mother was wonderfully decisive. She turned to the boy, cowering in a corner of the room, his head lowered and his hands clutched together in front of him, and shouted in Hindi: 'Get Dr Penrose – get him, now, now, hurry, *hurry*!' If he were not at home, then the boy should summon the young Geordie couple, the Roches, she added. She turned to us: 'Go to your room! At once! Both of you! And stay there – stay there till I tell you.'

Reluctantly we obeyed.

From our bedroom window – on the ground floor since this was a bungalow – we watched as Dr Penrose, usually leisurely and dignified in his pace, now dashed across the dusty space between his bungalow and ours. Soon the Roches also appeared. They must have already been having their siesta, since he was in only pyjamas and she in a dressing-gown.

Later young Dr Cameron, from the nearby military cantonment, drove up in his high, open-top Austin, from which, a notable athlete at both Fettes and Edinburgh University, he leapt down, to race towards the bungalow. After that we waited and waited, still standing at the window.

'Do you think he's dying?' Maria asked.

'Perhaps he's already dead.'

She shook her head violently, in a refusal to accept such an outcome.

'It must have been something he ate,' I said.

'Perhaps he has this – this cholera. He and mummy were talking about it yesterday. He went to see a patient in the bazaar. He thought that man had it. Remember?'

I nodded but it was the first that I had heard of this.

'People die of cholera,' she added. 'Very quickly. I remember nanny once told me that. She lived through a cholera epidemic in Bombay.'

'We don't get cholera. Only the Indians do.'

Eventually we saw Dr Cameron, Dr Penrose and Roche carrying our semi-conscious father out to the car, as though he were a bag of rubbish for the dump at the far end of the compound. Roche was supporting the shoulders, his teeth gritted with the effort. The other two were supporting the legs. At a distance, as though they dreaded that the calamity were somehow infectious, there cowered a small, huddled group of servants, among them the orderly, the boy *kitmatgar* and Dr Penrose's erect and white-bearded Muslim bearer, once an Indian Army sergeant. I remember briefly thinking it odd that there was no sign of Joseph. As the three Englishmen laid the body out in the back of the vehicle, I suddenly saw one of my father's legs first twitch convulsively and then kick out.

'He's alive! He's still alive!' I cried out.

Maria, hands to mouth, shook her head violently from side to side.

'Yes, he is! He is!'

My mother clambered into the back of the car, at the same time shifting my father's head and shoulders on to her lap. Dr Penrose carefully put a large foot on the running board and then heaved himself into the front passenger-seat. After some hesitation Roche squeezed himself in beside him, a hairy arm trailing outside the window.

For a moment I had a feeling of total abandonment. Then I heard Mrs Roche calling: 'Children! Children! Where are you? Are you all right?'

As we joined her, Maria asked: 'Where's Joseph? I didn't see Joseph.'

'Joseph?' Mrs Roche was puzzled.

'Our cook.'

'Oh, he's probably made himself scarce. Indians often do in an emergency.' She put an arm round Maria's shoulder and then stretched out her other arm to draw me close. 'You'd better come over to our bungalow until your mother gets back.'

I thought it ominous that she did not talk of our father also getting back.

He almost died; but, with his remarkable constitution, he somehow, against all the odds, survived. At first it was thought that, in that intense heat in a period without refrigerators, the chicken in his curry must have gone off. That would explain the mysterious disappearance of Joseph, who would no doubt have feared that he would be held responsible for the horror of what had occurred. None of the other servants, not even his boy assistant, would confess to having witnessed his departure. It was puzzling that Joseph had removed every one of his possessions, with the odd exception of the white shoes, perhaps considered by him to be too bulky to carry away along with everything else. My mother, with her usual brisk efficiency, was in search of a replacement cook as soon as she was no longer sleeping at the hospital and spending most of the hours of her days there.

Then came the devastating news. An analysis of my father's vomit and of the remaining curry in the dish from which only he had eaten, had revealed traces of poison. Who could possibly have wanted to kill my father? His was such a placid, benign nature and, though he could have easily become a successful physician in England, his religious convictions had instead sent him out to India to work largely among its most impoverished inhabitants in a climate that he hated. He was an innocent, almost a saint. Eventually it was generally agreed that, for some still mysterious reason, Joseph must have been responsible. It was he who had prepared the curry; and his immediate disappearance made his guilt all the more plausible.

Why, why, why? As he slowly recuperated, his face grey and oddly shiny and his voice reduced to a hoarse whisper, my father continually reverted to the question.

'*Pas devant les enfants,*' my mother would hiss. But she could not deter him.

'What did he have against me? What got into his head? I never did him any harm.'

On one occasion Roche, to whom these questions had been put when, unseen by the adults, I was reading an ancient copy of the *Illustrated London News* behind a bookcase in one corner of the sitting-room, replied 'He's probably a psychopath. No one can account for how such people behave.'

'But he always seemed so normal. And so decent. I never doubted the sincerity of his beliefs, never for one moment.'

Then, when my father was once more able to resume his work and my mother was about to take my sister and myself at long last up to Naina Tal, the answer came. A CID officer, a small man with a sharp profile and slightly protuberant teeth, visited us with some news. What it was, Maria and I, banished to our bedroom, did not hear in person. But we learned of it later. Investigations had revealed that Joseph had never worked for a mission in Lucknow. His references must have been forged. He had been identified, by means of some photographs taken by our mother of him and us two children together in the garden, in the kitchen and outside his hut He was a well-known agitator and member of a secret society, recently inflitrated by the Intelligence Bureau, called The Red Arrow. The group had been responsible for four attempted assassinations and one successful one. Apparently – I learned this many years later from my father – the CID officer had expressed contempt that Joseph's efforts to 'bump off' (his phrase) my father, had been so inefficient. The idiot, the officer said, had not realised that the poison would have been so much diluted by the curry with which it was mixed that it could not be relied on to be lethal. 'They rarely get it right. Hopeless.'

'Well, thank God for that,' was my father's reply. Then he asked: 'But why was I his target? Why pick on me? I've nothing to do with the government. I'm a person of no importance.'

'Well, we have a theory about that. There's someone with the same name of yours in the Intelligence Bureau. Not merely surname, Christian name too. Did you know that? Yours is not a usual surname. Is it?' He laughed. 'Oh, trust them to get something like that wrong! We're pretty sure that that's what it was.'

It was soon after we had returned to the mission, the hot weather over, that there was another piece of news. Joseph had been involved in the attempted assassination of an Indian prominent in the Viceroy's Council. An informer had given warning, so that the chauffeured car in which the Indian politician had been supposed to set out had contained not him but a police officer, and a police officer had also taken the place of the usual chauffeur. Another car, containing armed policemen in mufti, had followed. All the six members of the assassination squad had been machine-gunned to death as they had tried to escape from the cordon around them.

I remember how Maria, my mother and I listened in an increasingly oppressive silence to my father recounting all this to us. We had just arrived back in the house, late in the evening, and the dining-room was feebly lit by two oil-lamps and an acetyline one, dangling from the ceiling, on which it cast huge shadows. Had those shadows really seemed horribly menacing to me, the nine-year-old child that I then was, or is it creative memory that has now persuaded me that they did?

I was looking at my father, not at either my mother or Maria. 'One can't help feeling sorry for the poor devil,' my father said at the close of his narration.

'*Sorry*! How can you feel sorry?' my mother demanded, her face suddenly growing red. Her voice, usually so reasonable and quiet, now rasped with fury. 'What a fool you are! How can you feel sorry for a thug who tried to kill you? Oh, you make me sick, you really make me sick!'

'But we're told to love our enemies and to do good to those who hate us. Aren't we? Isn't that what we believe?' My father's voice was plaintive.

'Oh, for heaven's sake!' my mother shouted. I had never before witnessed her show such contempt for my father.

'Anyway ...' Calmly my father got to his feet and walked over to his desk. 'Here's a last photograph.' He picked up a copy of *The Times of India*, folded back at a page. 'A photograph of him.' He held it out to us. 'Horrible. Why do they publish such things?'

Suddenly, with astonishing speed, Maria leapt up from her chair and raced over to where he was standing. She snatched the newspaper and stared down at it. Later, I too was to stare down at it and examine, with a mixture of revulsion and triumph, the half-page, black-and-white photograph of the body lying out on a pavement, with a crowd of people jostling around it, as three Indian policemen in uniform struggled to hold them back. Joseph's white cotton trousers and long shirt were blotched with dark stains. His head was twisted sideways. There was a triangle of blood beneath it, and in the centre of one cheek there gaped a dark, jagged hole. A turban lay beside a clenched hand.

Maria glared in turn at each of us. Then she let out an extraordinary yelp, as of an animal caught in a trap from which it cannot escape. My mother tried to grab her arm as she loped, body almost doubled over, out of the room.

'Maria! Maria!' my mother called. Then she demanded: 'What's come over the child?'

'She was fond of him,' I said. But that did not seem, even then, an adequate reason for such an outburst.

'I expect she's tired after that ghastly journey,' my mother said. 'I certainly am. Let's see if Mohammed can rustle something up for us to eat.'

Mohammed was our new cook. Next morning my father would be complaining of his 'inedible' scrambled eggs – but would nonetheless eat them.

3

When in the past I have performed this task of clearing up the debris of a life that has ended – my mother's, my father's, a cousin's, this or that friend's – I have became less and less discriminating and more and more impatient. In consequence, my pace has constantly accelerated. So it is now. Who would want this almost new dressing-gown, this folding umbrella, this long rope of chunky amber beads? Who would be glad to be given a hagiography of Lenin printed in East Germany, a copy of *Whitacker's Almanack* dated 1983, or a hot-water bottle in a pale-blue cover presumably crocheted by Maria herself? All these I thrust, without hesitation, into one of the black bin bags that Mrs Bird (or Bard or Baird) has given me for the things that I decide not to keep and that she says that she will eventually pass on to the local equivalent of the RSPCA.

Maria's life was so full of passion, ardour and endeavour. She organised CND sit-downs, she camped out on Greenham Common, she invaded Rugby pitches to demonstrate against South African teams playing in Britain. She wrote innumerable letters to newspapers, few of them ever published. She sent countless cheques to human-rights organisations, some genuine like Amnesty and Index on Censorship, but many merely disseminators of propaganda for this or that Communist regime.

Now I am turning the pages of her passport. It is crammed with the blurred stamps of countries that few tourists would ever dream of entering, so dangerous and backward are they. With a sigh, I consign it to yet another overflowing bin bag. How strange and how sad that all that is left of so much selfless, if also self-deluding, activity should now be contained in these five or six plastic bags stacked against each other in a corner of a single narrow, stifling room. How sad and strange, too, that all the money that our German grandmother so carefully husbanded in her Swiss bank account and left in its entirety to her favourite grandchild, should have then been recklessly squandered on causes that, if they had achieved the worldwide success of which Maria had so obsessively dreamed and for which she had so persistently fought, would have made obsolete all private accumulations of capital.

I am nearing the end of my task when I notice that far under the bed, almost out of sight, there lies a battered brief-case. Half-kneeling – I feel a sudden, sharp twinge in my right knee as I stoop – I reach under the bed and drag it out. At some time Maria, who was always losing her keys, must have forced the lock, so that its hasp is broken and the briefcase is fastened only by one of its two straps. I open it. It has three compartments.

In one of these compartments there is a yellowing cutting from *The Daily Worker*. When I unfold it, it reveals a long obituary of the Indian nationalist politican Subhash Chandra Bose, repeatedly imprisoned by the Raj for his attempts, then regarded as traitorous, to ally India with the Japanese and Germans during the War. Maria has underlined certain phrases in red ink – 'burning idealism', 'unflinching courage', 'a moral beacon', 'selfless in his pursuit of …' I read no further. I screw the cutting up in a fist and then throw it towards one of the black bags. It falls to one side of it and then, as though it had a life of its own, slowly, flower-like, begins to uncurl in the dry wind from the open window above it.

The second compartment of the briefcase contains, to my amazement, nothing but a clearly ancient pessary. I always assumed Maria to have been a virgin, too much in love with causes and humanity at large to focus sexually on any single human being, male or female. I push it back into the briefcase.

In the third compartment I come on an ancient sponge-bag. There is something hard inside it. A dried-out piece of soap? I unzip it. No. It's that piece of wood carved by Joseph to decorate Maria's and my birthday cake more than seventy years ago. I stare down at it, with a mingling of amazement and, yes, annihilating grief, of a kind that the news of Maria's death has failed until this moment to cause me. Inseparably – like Siamese, not ordinary, twins – our figures are conjoined. The sunny smiles that Joseph carved on to our faces now look to me like rictuses of agony. The shirt that he long ago painted a bright blue has faded, some of its colour drained away in irregular streaks. Only Maria's strap-shoes are still pristine. They look far too large for the tiny figure to which they are attached.

I continue to gaze down at the object. How strange that for all these years, during which she recklessly jettisoned her family, her inherited fortune and our bewildered parents' hopes that she would achieve a conventional career or a conventional marriage, she nevertheless kept this piece of wood picked up from under a banyan tree in an obscure, overgrown Indian garden and then inexpertly carved by a murderer.

Slowly I put the conjoined figures into the pocket of my crumpled, ill-fitting linen jacket, making it bulge and so look, I am sure, even more unsightly. As I move, the irregular object, with its sharp protuberances of heads and elbows, digs into my thigh.

'How are you getting on?' Her voice sounds vaguely impatient. Perhaps I have overstayed my welcome. 'Your taxi is here.'

'My taxi?'

I have forgotten that the driver of the taxi that brought me here insisted that he would pick me to up to take me back to my hotel. There are few tourists in Luxor now and the trade is therefore highly competitive.

'I told the driver to wait. He won't charge a fortune for doing so, as in London.'

'I'm almost finished.'

'Don't worry about the bags and boxes. My husband can carry them out to the station wagon when he gets home. We can drop them off tomorrow — the ones you want at your hotel, the rest at that charity. He has an almost free day and, thank God, I've finished that wretched commission. I could paint those pictures in my sleep.'

The taxi moves slowly along the corniche in the dying light of a sun that seems to rest, an enormous, immoveable disk, above the sterile, humped mountains. Since my responses have been so grudging, the driver has now stopped his exuberant chatter. I gaze at the sauntering crowds. I put a hand into my jacket pocket and touch the two figures. I touch them again. Then I draw them out and stare down at them. Again I am overwhelmed by that feeling of mingled revulsion and annihilating sadness.

On an impulse, I suddenly lean across the cracked, dusty seat towards the window open beside me, and fling the ancient relic out into the road. I turn my head, feeling faintly dizzy as I do so, and look back at it through the rear window. A vast lorry passes over it without doing it any damage as it turns off the corniche. Then two ramshackle cars, clearly racing each other and almost touching, speed up to pass us. The wheel of one goes over it and crushes it, as it might an empty cigarette packet or a plastic bottle.

I lean my head back and close my eyes. I long for silence, for my air-conditioned room, for my bed, and for that blissful state when, suspended in a fragile hammock between retreating life and approaching death, all remembrance and even all thinking cease.